PUFFIN BOOKS
ESCAPE FROM JAVA AND OTHER TALES OF DANGER

Born in Kasauli (Himachal Pradesh) in 1934, Ruskin Bond grew up in Jamnagar (Gujarat), Dehra Dun, New Delhi and Simla. His first novel, *The Room on the Roof*, written when he was seventeen, won the John Llewellyn Rhys Memorial Prize in 1957. Since then he has written over three hundred short stories, essays and novellas (including *Vagrants in the Valley*, *A Flight of Pigeons* and *Delhi Is Not Far*), and more than fifty books for children.

He has also written numerous articles that have appeared in a number of magazines and anthologies. He received the Sahitya Akademi Award in 1993 and the Padma Shri in 1999. Several of his stories have been filmed, including *The Blue Umbrella*, *A Flight of Pigeons* (filmed as *Junoon*), and *Susanna's Seven Husbands* (as a forthcoming film *Saath Khoon Maaf*).

He lives in Landour, Mussoorie, with his extended family.

Escape from Java and Other Tales of Danger

RUSKIN BOND

Illustrated by
Priya Kurian

PUFFIN BOOKS

PUFFIN BOOKS
Published by the Penguin Group
Penguin Books India Pvt. Ltd, 11 Community Centre, Panchsheel Park,
New Delhi 110 017, India
Penguin Group (USA) Inc., 375 Hudson Street, New York, New York 10014,
USA
Penguin Group (Canada), 90 Eglinton Avenue East, Suite 700, Toronto,
Ontario, M4P 2Y3, Canada (a division of Pearson Penguin Canada Inc.)
Penguin Books Ltd, 80 Strand, London WC2R 0RL, England
Penguin Ireland, 25 St Stephen's Green, Dublin 2, Ireland (a division of
Penguin Books Ltd)
Penguin Group (Australia), 250 Camberwell Road, Camberwell, Victoria
3124, Australia (a division of Pearson Australia Group Pty Ltd)
Penguin Group (NZ), 67 Apollo Drive, Rosedale, North Shore 0632,
New Zealand (a division of Pearson New Zealand Ltd)
Penguin Group (South Africa) (Pty) Ltd, 24 Sturdee Avenue, Rosebank,
Johannesburg 2196, South Africa

Penguin Books Ltd, Registered Offices: 80 Strand, London WC2R 0RL,
England

First published in Puffin by Penguin Books India 2010

Text copyright © Ruskin Bond 2010
Illustrations copyright © Priya Kurian 2010

The novella *Earthquake* was first published by Julia MacRae Books, London, 1984
'Riding through the Flames', 'Escape from Java' and 'Sita and the River'
were published in *Dust on the Mountains: Collected Stories*, Penguin Books
India, 1996
The novella *A Flight of Pigeons* was first published in Viking by Penguin Books
India, 2002

All rights reserved

10 9 8 7 6 5 4 3 2 1

ISBN 9780143331346

Typeset in Sabon MT by Eleven Arts, Keshav Puram, New Delhi 110035

Printed at Manipal Press Ltd.

Contents

Earthquake

Grandfather's Bath

Whenever there was an emergency, Grandfather happened to be in his bath.

He was in his bath when a wild elephant smashed its way through the garden, trampling Grandmother's prize roses and sweet peas and bringing down the garden wall. He was in his bath when the roof of the house blew away in a cyclone. And he was in his bath when a visiting aunt went into hysterics because there was a baby python curled up on her dressing table. On all these occasions he expressed surprise that anything could have happened during the twenty minutes he was in his bathtub; by the time he had dressed, everything was over—the wild elephant had gone trumpeting on its way, the cyclonic storm had passed, and the baby python had been removed by young master Rakesh who had put it there in the first place.

Grandfather's bath consisted of an old-fashioned tin tub filled with several buckets of hot water to which he added sprigs of mint. A mint bath! No one had ever heard of such a thing, but Grandfather said it was most refreshing.

Grandfather sang in his bath and splashed around a lot, which is probably why he seldom knew what was going on elsewhere.

He was in his bath when the first shock of the great earthquake shook north-eastern India, an earthquake that was to reduce most of the town to rubble.

The family (or most of it) was living in Shillong, a busy little town in the Cherrapunji Hills, where Grandfather Burman had retired after leaving the Forest Service. He'd bought a large old house on the outskirts of the town, a house so large and so old that most of his pension was used up in constantly repairing it. Grandmother Burman just about managed to make both ends meet. There were no servants except for Mumtaz, a cook who'd been with the family since Grandfather's forest service days; he had four small children of his own.

The Burman's grandchildren lived with them. Rakesh, eleven, rode off to school on his bicycle every morning. Mukesh, six, refused to go to school until he was seven. Dolly, three, followed Grandmother about the house and garden, helping her feed the chickens and the dog (which was half a dachshund and half a spaniel and was called Pickle) and a goat that Grandfather insisted would provide them with milk some day—only so far it hadn't.

The children's mother had died when Dolly was born; and their father, Mr Burman, worked on a tea estate a few hundred miles away, where there were no schools. So the children stayed with Mr Burman's parents, who wouldn't have parted with them for anything in the world.

Every year there were earth tremors in this part of India, but there hadn't been a really big earthquake for thirty years.

'What do you do when there's an earthquake?' asked Rakesh, who had heard all about the last one.

'There isn't time to do much,' said Grandfather. 'Everyone just rushes out of doors.'

'I'll stay in my bed until it's over,' said Rakesh.

'I'll get *under* my bed,' said Mukesh. 'It can't find me there!'

'It's best to stand in a doorway,' said Grandmother. 'If you look at earthquake pictures, you'll notice that the door frames are always left standing!'

Although Shillong was in a region where earthquakes sometimes happened, the family liked living there.

There was a lake and a colourful bazaar, and Grandmother's garden was full of butterflies, birds and exotic orchids, as well as fruit trees and trees that were fun to climb. Rakesh liked roaming around the town on his bicycle. Mukesh enjoyed the sweet shops in the bazaar—when he wasn't wrestling in the dust with Mumtaz's two boys. Dolly kept herself busy building her own doll's house under the suitcase.

Life moved at a gentle pace in Shillong. Apart from the elephant in the garden, nothing very exciting had happened recently to the family. The highlight of the year had been Rakesh's winning the high jump in his school sports, for which he had won a small cup—so small, that he had given it to Dolly to add to her doll's house.

Then one morning, while Grandfather was having his bath, the town seemed suddenly very still and very quiet . . .

The First Tremors

Grandfather didn't notice anything because he was splashing about and singing; but Grandmother, who was in the garden trimming her rose bushes, paused in her work and looked up. Why were the birds silent all of a sudden? Not only the birds in the trees, but the birds in the hen-house too. And the goat had stopped nibbling at the geraniums. And the dog, who had been yapping at a squirrel on the wall, sat down quietly, ears back, head between his paws.

'Now isn't that funny,' said Grandmother aloud. 'I wonder what . . .'

And then the opposite happened. The hens began cackling, the dogs barking, and the birds shrieking and flapping their wings. The crows in the neighbourhood all took wing, wheeling wildly overhead and cawing loudly. The chickens flapped around in circles, as if they were being chased. Two cats sitting on the wall suddenly jumped up and disappeared in opposite directions.

Grandmother had read somewhere that animals sense the approach of an earthquake much quicker than humans. And true enough, within half a minute of her noticing the noise made by the animals, she heard a rattling, rumbling sound, like the approach of an express train.

The noise increased for about a minute and then there was the first trembling of the ground. The animals by this time all seemed to have gone mad and were making a hideous noise. Treetops lashed backwards and forwards, doors banged and windows shook, and Grandmother said later that the house actually swayed in front of her. She had difficulty in stranding straight, although she admitted that this may have been due more to the trembling of her knees than to the trembling of the ground.

This first shock lasted only about half a minute, but it seemed much longer. Grandmother realized that Grandfather was in his bath, that Rakesh was on his way to school, that Mukesh was playing marbles with Mumtaz's son, and that Dolly was under the staircase busy with her doll's house; Mumtaz would be in the kitchen washing vegetables. Grandmother rushed indoors to fetch Dolly.

As she did so, the rumble grew louder. Grandfather did not hear it because he was still singing; but Grandmother heard it, and so did Dolly, who also noticed that her doll's house was beginning to totter. Along with the rumble, Mumtaz heard the rattle of crockery. A teapot slithered off the sideboard and fell to the floor in pieces. In the sitting room, an antique vase (three hundred years old, according to Grandfather), leapt off the mantelpiece and crashed to the ground.

When Dolly felt the first tremor, she instinctively crawled under the well of the staircase, dragging her favourite doll with her. All the doll's hair had long since come out, and so had one eye, but Dolly had had the doll a long time and felt she needed special care and attention. She couldn't understand why the house was shaking, but she wasn't afraid. Houses just shook sometimes, she supposed.

Grandmother did not see her under the staircase and dashed into the drawing room, calling, 'Dolly, Dolly! Where are you?' The clocks on the wall went crazy and began striking all hours.

In the kitchen, Mumtaz was trying to catch plates, glasses and dishes as they sprang madly from the shelves. Mukesh had lost all his marbles, and not in a game with his friends. They had rolled out of the gate and down the road and then disappeared into the ground, where a number of fissures had appeared.

Grandfather stopped singing when he found he couldn't manage the high notes. He noticed that his bathtub was almost empty. Surely he hadn't splashed so much! He reached for the mug, but couldn't find it. He started getting out of the tub, but the tub itself rose up and pitched him out on the flooded bathroom floor.

'A ghost!' exclaimed Grandfather. 'There's a mischievous ghost in here, playing tricks with the tub!'

He grabbed his towel and wrapped it round his waist, then flung open the bathroom door and dashed on to the landing.

By that time the first earthquake tremor was over.

* * *

Rakesh was halfway to school when he found his cycle swerving about on the road, out of his control. He almost collided with a bullock cart.

He dismounted to see if the cycle-chain had jammed. He found the road as unsteady as the bicycle! But this sensation lasted for just a few seconds. Everything was steady again.

Strangely, though, the bullocks were refusing to move on.

'Did you feel that?' asked the cart driver.

'Yes, everything was shaking,' said Rakesh. 'Was it an earthquake?'

'A small one,' said the driver. 'Or the start of a big one!'

Rakesh rode on to school. The bell had yet to ring for classes, and the field was a ferment of excitement, as the assembled boys and girls stood around in groups talking about the shock that had just been felt. The headmaster had decided that, just in case there was another tremor, the children would be safer out in the open than in the rather ancient school building; and so he delayed the ringing of the assembly bell. Naturally the children were delighted at the delay. But when nothing further happened after fifteen minutes, the headmaster decided it was time for school. There were groans of protest, followed by calls for a holiday. Rakesh was the spokesman for his class.

'Sir, you gave us a holiday last year when the roof blew off!'

'But the roof has not blown off,' observed the headmaster.

'What if the walls fall down, sir?'

'When the walls fall, we will think about a holiday,' snapped the headmaster. 'Now into class all of you!'

Earthquake Gossip

'Couldn't have a proper bath,' grumbled Grandfather. 'There wasn't enough water in the tub!'

'Didn't you feel it?' asked Grandmother.

'Feel what?'

'The earthquake.'

'Didn't feel a thing. You must have imagined it.'

'Well, most of the crockery is broken, as well as that vase you brought back from Burma. You can eat your lunch out of a banana leaf, or use Dolly's toy tea set.'

'Where are Mukesh and Dolly?'

'Dolly's under the staircase again. It's her favourite place. Mukesh is playing outside with Mumtaz's biggest boy. That tremor didn't seem to bother them. But I hope that shock didn't cause any damage at Rakesh's school.'

'Couldn't have . . . we hardly felt it.'

'*You* never notice anything when you're in the bath. Everyone else felt it—including the hens! They've suffered nervous breakdowns and won't lay eggs for days.'

Going round the house, Grandmother noticed several cracks in the walls and pointed them out to Grandfather.

'They were there before,' said Grandfather.

'They've been there for years.'

'Well, I hadn't noticed them before. Anyway, it's time we left this house. It's much too big and costs too much to look after.'

'I suppose we can settle in Calcutta. But you won't enjoy living in a small flat. And you're not used to the crowds.'

'I was thinking of another hill station—where they don't have earthquakes. We could sell this place and buy or rent a cottage in Darjeeling or Kalimpong.'

'Then pray we don't have another earthquake,' said Grandfather. 'No one's going to buy a ruin.'

They heard Mukesh shouting in the garden.

'He's up to some mischief as usual,' grumbled Grandmother, going out to see what all the noise was about.

Mukesh had found a nest and several broken eggs on the lawn, and was shouting because he was being attacked by a pair of angry thrushes.

'What did you do to that nest?' demanded Grandmother.

'Nothing!' said Mukesh. 'It fell out of the trees when everything began to shake!'

'That must have been what happened. But keep away from the nest, or those birds will really go for you!'

The dog Pickle had been running about looking for whoever had caused all the commotion. He and the neighbour's dog began barking at each other, as though laying the blame at each other's doorsteps. 'How dare you rock my house!' they seemed to be saying. Eventually tiring of the argument, Pickle went into the storeroom looking for rats. He was good at catching rats.

* * *

In the town everyone was talking about the tremor that had just been felt. As there hadn't been any serious damage and nothing big had fallen down, it was all thought to have been great fun. But there were older people who remembered the earthquake of thirty years ago, and who had lost friends, relatives and homes when hundreds of houses had fallen down. They knew that a mild earthquake tremor was often followed by a second, more severe shock—and they dreaded this possibility. There was talk of the jail collapsing and the prisoners escaping; of the mighty Brahmaputra river changing its course and flooding the whole of Assam, while crocodiles invaded the towns and villages; of glaciers sliding down from the Himalayas; and of the earth opening up and swallowing the whole of Shillong!

'The end of the world is near!' proclaimed a holy man in the bazaar.

'Tell us, holy one, what should we do about it?' asked a shopkeeper.

'Purify yourself,' said the holy man. 'Take care of your soul!'

'In other words,' said a passing wit, 'don't cheat your customers.'

'And when did *you* ever work for a living,' shouted the shopkeeper. 'You still owe me twenty rupees!'

Back at the Burman house, the family sat down to a quiet lunch. It wasn't quiet for long, because Dolly wanted what was on Mukesh's plate (even though it was no different from hers), and when she was told to eat her own food, she threw a tantrum.

'These *children*,' sighed Rakesh, bolting down his rice and bean curry. 'It's time they went to school.'

'It's time *you* got back to school,' said Grandmother. 'It's half past one.'

'We're not having school this afternoon. Although we couldn't get an earthquake-holiday, we're going to watch the cricket match. There's a team from Calcutta playing against the Lake Club.'

'Take me with you,' said Mukesh.

'No, you're always falling off the back of the cycle.'

'I'll sit in front, then.'

'You'll stay at home,' said Grandmother. 'The last time you went to a football match, you got lost.'

'But this is a cricket match,' argued Mukesh. 'No one gets lost at cricket matches.'

'Would you like to come with me to the Bengali sweet shop?' asked Grandfather.

'Oh, please,' said Mukesh. 'It's better than cricket. Better than that rotten bicycle.'

'Why do we have earthquakes?' asked Rakesh.

'Well,' said Grandfather, 'the earth has been around a long time—millions of years—and sometimes it feels the stress and strain of being so old . . .'

'Are you a million?' interrupted Mukesh.

'Not yet,' said Grandfather, 'not yet. But, just like me, the earth wants to stretch a little and yawn, and when it does, the earth's crust has these convulsions— we call them earthquakes.'

'But why does it have to stretch *here*?' asked Rakesh.

'It can stretch anywhere, and *does*. Tokyo, San Francisco, Iran, the South Pacific, Italy, Turkey— there's hardly a corner of the earth that hasn't felt an earthquake at some time or the other. Of course in some places it's worse . . . This is one of the places where the earth likes to do its stretching.'

When lunch was over, Rakesh rode off to the cricket ground, Grandfather and Mukesh walked off in the direction of the bazaar, and Dolly followed

Grandmother into the courtyard to help with the washing.

It was about ten minutes later that the real earthquake was felt, and half the town came tumbling down.

Earthquake Chaos

Rakesh had almost reached the cricket ground when, all of a sudden, the road tilted and rose up towards him. A second later he found himself sprawling on the ground.

A deep rumbling sound seemed to come from the bowels of the earth, and the road kept having convulsions. It was like a huge snake thrashing around in its death throes. Rakesh found that lying on the ground was even more difficult than riding his bicycle.

The cricket match, which had started a little while earlier, came to an abrupt end, as a huge rent appeared across the pitch. Into it fell a fast bowler, an umpire, and a fielder standing at silly mid-on. They were rescued later, but it was the first time anywhere that a match had to be abandoned due to an earthquake.

Those who were playing, or watching from the lakeside pavilion, heard a thunderous roar. It was due to half the hillside falling into the lake. The earth, along with trees, bushes and rocks, simply bulged out, and then came crashing down. Dust and water rose skywards, and at the same time the bed of the lake erupted, rose like a tidal wave, and spewed its contents over the surrounding plain. Fortunately for both cricketers and spectators, this massive surge of water was flowing in the opposite direction. But it swept away a number of parked cars, several grazing cattle and goats, telegraph poles, and the walls of the old jail.

Here was a chance for hundreds of inmates of the jail to escape. But they were too shocked by the suddenness of the disaster to be able to do anything except make a dash for the high ground behind the jail. A few could not make it and were washed away by the rushing waters of the upturned lake. Those who reached safety huddled together in groups, waiting to be rescued.

Rakesh saw the wave coming towards him as he lay on the ground. It was about fifty metres away when he scrambled to his feet and ran for the nearest tree. Fortunately it was a large banyan tree, well anchored with its many aerial roots—branches that had come down to the ground and taken root again. It was also an easy tree to climb. Rakesh climbed as high as he could go, glancing down as the advancing water swirled around beneath him. He watched as his bicycle swept past. And he was never to see it again.

* * *

Grandfather and Mukesh were in the bazaar, eating sweets. They both shared a passion for gulab-jamuns—rose-scented milk and sugar dumplings fried a deep brown. The old man and the small boy stood outside the sweet shop popping syrupy gulab-jamuns down their throats.

The bazaar itself was a hive of activity. It was the busiest hour of the day. The street was crowded with women shopping for vegetables, and pavement-vendors selling everything from shiny brassware to old clothes and second-hand comics, in competition with the bigger shops just off the road. Weaving in and out of the crowd were cyclists, scooterists, pony carts, stray cows, stray dogs and even stray policemen.

Mukesh had eaten four gulab-jamuns and Grandfather six when the sweet shop began to wobble about in front of them. Then the cloth awning collapsed, burying the shopkeeper among his

sweetmeats. His muffled shouts for help were lost in the noise from the street, where people were shouting and rushing about in panic.

Grandfather and Mukesh found themselves on top of the struggling shopkeeper. As he freed himself, Mukesh got stuck in the awning and had to be helped out, and all the time the ground was heaving about and shops were tottering and collapsing like packs of cards.

In the space of a few seconds, a straight bazaar had become a crooked bazaar. The road had been twisted out of shape to such an extent that some shops that had been on the left now turned up on the right, and vice versa. A beggar in a cart who had never been known to walk now leapt to his feet and ran for his life. The cows had vanished and so had the policemen. A motorcycle had disappeared into a hole in the ground, while a car had mounted the steps of the Town Hall. A tonga-pony galloped down the middle of the road; of the tonga and its driver there was no sign.

The Town Hall itself had collapsed, burying a number of clerks and officials. By the time the powerful tremor had passed, several other large buildings had also come down.

Grandfather did not panic. He picked Mukesh off a heap of sweets and helped the dazed shopkeeper to his feet. Then he realized that the earthquake must have affected every part of the town.

'Let's get back to the house,' he said. 'Anything could have happened!'

Grabbing Mukesh by the hand, he started running down the road. Mukesh had trouble keeping up with him. He'd never seen Grandfather running before.

* * *

Dolly was helping Grandmother hang out the washing when the shock came. Had they been inside the house, they would not have come out alive.

As in the case of the first tremor, the dog began to howl and all the birds rose from the trees and began circling overhead, making a great noise. Then suddenly there was a wind rushing through the trees, and the ground began to heave and quake.

Dolly looked up to see the tall chimney toppling off the roof of the house.

'Look, Granny!' she cried. 'The house is falling down! What will happen to my doll's house?'

'Never mind the doll's house,' said Grandmother. 'Let's get clear of the building.'

They ran into the garden just as the walls of the house bulged outwards and the roof fell inwards.

There was a great crash, followed by clouds of dust and plaster.

Grandmother looked across the road and saw other houses collapsing, almost as though some unseen giant was blowing them all down. The lines from an English fairy tale ran through her head: 'I'll huff and puff and I'll blow your house down!'

There was a peculiar whistling wind, but it wasn't the wind that had done the damage; it was the quivering of the earth that had loosened bricks and plaster, beams and rafters. The air was filled with choking dust. They couldn't speak.

How flimsy all the houses seem, thought Grandmother. Just dolls' houses. And yet, many of them had stood for over a hundred years. A hundred years—and in a moment, gone!

The shaking had stopped, but already their home was a mound of rubble. A bedstead poked out of a broken window. A bathroom tap gushed water over a squashed sofa set. Here a bit of broken desk or chair, there a bit of torn carpet, a familiar hat, battered books, a twisted umbrella; these were the only reminders that this had once been a home.

The goat was missing, the hens had vanished. The only things that hadn't been touched were the clothes that Dolly and Grandmother had been hanging up. They remained firmly on the washing line, flapping about in the wind.

Cries from afar came to them on the wind—cries for help, people calling out for each other, some just shouting because there was nothing else to do.

Dolly and Grandmother stood like statues in the middle of the garden. They were too shocked to move—until they saw Grandfather and Mukesh running down the road towards them. Then they too began to run.

Pickle found himself trapped in the storeroom. He had been ferreting between two large boxes, trying to get at a terrified rat, when the ceiling came down on top of the boxes. There was dust and darkness everywhere. Pickle didn't like it one bit. He wanted to be out of that suffocating hole, and he wasn't going to sit there waiting to be rescued. The instincts of the dachshund, and his own experience in digging for rats, now came to his aid. He began burrowing in the rubble, trying to tunnel a way out.

The Lucky Ones

Mumtaz's hut was one of the few homes left standing. Light and flimsy and made of wooden planks and a thatched roof, it could have been blown away by a strong wind. But it withstood the earthquake. Whereas bricks and plaster had come crashing down, the light wooden structure had shaken and shivered and swayed with the movements of the earth, but it had remained upright.

Dolly was soon at home in the hut, playing on the smooth earthen floor with the cook's children. Mukesh still hung on to Grandfather, while Grandmother, hands on hips, surveyed the wreckage of the house.

'I hope Rakesh is all right,' said Grandfather.

'If you can keep an eye on Mukesh, I'll go and look for him.'

'Yes, do. I'm worried about him,' said Grandmother. 'And we may get another earthquake.'

'Will you be all right here?'

'Well, there's nothing left to fall down. Mumtaz says we must sleep in his house tonight. It seems to be the safest place.'

'You and the children can sleep there. I'll sleep out in the open. It's warm enough—and I don't think it will rain.'

While Grandfather was gone looking for Rakesh, Grandmother and Mumtaz searched the ruins of the house, looking for things that could still be used. Unfortunately most of their belongings were buried deep beneath the rubble, and there was hardly anything worth retrieving—just a battered pram, a boxful of clothes, several tins of sardines, some cans of fruit juice that had rolled across the grass, and Grandfather's typewriter, which hadn't been working anyway. They had no idea that Pickle was in the ruined building, buried at the bottom of everything; they thought he was somewhere in the neighbourhood, dashing about as usual, looking for the cause of all the trouble.

'Find my dolls!' demanded Dolly. 'And the doll's house.'

But the doll's house no longer existed.

'No more toys,' said Mukesh with satisfaction, feeling very grown-up about everything. 'We're *poor* now.'

'Has the bank fallen down too?' asked Dolly.

'Must have,' said Mukesh sagely.

In spite of Grandfather's prediction of clear weather, it began to rain and they had to take shelter in Mumtaz's little hut. It was very crowded in the small room, but Mumtaz, for one, did not notice—he had a big heart.

* * *

The waters of the upturned lake drained away almost as rapidly as they had flooded the surrounding area. Rakesh peered through the branches of the tree in the general direction of his school. He wanted to know the time. Usually the clock tower above the school building was visible for miles around, but now there was no sign of it. It had, in fact, disappeared when the rest of the building collapsed. Even now, frantic efforts were being made to extricate the headmaster from the rubble around his desk, where he had been trapped by a falling beam. The classrooms were a shambles and a fire had broken out in the kitchen and was spreading to other parts of the building. It would be many months before the school would start functioning again. Many would never return to it.

After some time Rakesh climbed down from the tree. He looked around for his bicycle, but couldn't see it anywhere. A lot of other things had been washed up at the base of the tree, including a dead cat, several drowned chickens, fish that had been left flopping around when the water receded, and a cinema hoarding. The face of a famous Bombay film star stared up from the mud.

In the distance he saw a great cloud of dust. He did not know it then, but the dust came from hundreds of fallen or damaged buildings. Rakesh knew, of course, that there had been an earthquake, and a tremendous one, and that it must have been felt over a large area. What could have happened to his grandparents and his brother and sister? He began running for home, taking the road through the town.

He wasn't sure it was the same town he was running through, because many of the familiar landmarks had gone. The town's biggest and most expensive hotel, the Grand Eastern, had tumbled down. Many of its guests had been killed. An ambulance stood in the grounds, and across the road a fire engine was trying to put out several fires which had broken out. Almost automatically Rakesh began to help the rescue workers who were clearing the rubble. There wasn't much he could do apart from shifting bricks and broken furniture. Then he realized that his own home might be in a similar condition, and he paused, staring horrified at the wreckage of the once posh hotel. He felt a touch on his shoulder. Grandfather was standing beside him.

'Are you all right, my boy?'

Rakesh nodded, although he looked rather bewildered.

'And everyone at home?' he asked.

'They're all right.' Grandfather did not mention the house. 'Come along, there's nothing you can do here. What happened to the bicycle?'

'It was swept away. All the water came out of the lake. I had to climb a tree!'

They walked home in silence. But all around them there was noise and confusion.

Rakesh hadn't expected to find their house in total ruin. He looked around in shock and dismay.

'Everything's gone,' he said at last. 'What luck—what terrible luck . . .'

'No,' said Grandfather. 'We're the *lucky* ones! We're alive, aren't we?'

Beginning Again

Late that night, Grandfather wondered if he had spoken too soon. There was another strong tremor, and Mumtaz's frail hut swayed and swung as though it was a hot-air balloon. In the town, more buildings came down.

Grandfather had been wrong about the weather too, because it did not stop raining and he had to give up his plan to sleep outside. Everyone else had bedded down on the floor of the hut, using bits of torn carpet and bedding rescued from the house. It was a tight squeeze, with Mumtaz and his wife and four small children taking up half the space, and Grandmother and the family taking up the other half. Nobody slept much, except for Mukesh and the smaller children.

In the middle of the night, Pickle finally succeeded in digging his way out of the ruins. He was white with plaster, and one of his long ears had almost come off. He sat down outside the hut and howled for most of the night. Other dogs in other parts of the town took up the howling, so it was a weird, frightening sort of night, what with the wind, the rain, the howling—and always the fear of another earth tremor.

Grandfather had noticed that although the hut swayed about when there was a tremor, it showed no signs of falling down—unlike the big brick and stone buildings that had come down so quickly. Indeed, although they did not know it then, almost everything made of brick and masonry had been levelled to the ground. Wooden structures, no matter how rickety, had withstood the earthquake.

The full extent of the damage would not be known for a few days, because the earthquake had been felt all over Assam and parts of Bengal. A train had overturned at one place, while another left the rails. Over a thousand people lost their lives in the Cherrapunji Hills. The mighty Brahmaputra river burst its banks and many farmers were drowned in the flood. In one small town, two elephants sat down in the bazaar and refused to get up until the following morning. One man was lucky; when the walls of his house came down, a pot of coins showered down on him. But no one else found any treasure.

It rained all night, and although the main shock of the earthquake had passed, minor shocks took place at regular intervals of five minutes or so. Rakesh stayed awake with the grown-ups. He was sure the school buildings had fallen, and there wouldn't be school for months. There wouldn't be much else, either.

Early in the morning, Mumtaz got up to make tea on his small primus stove. Grandfather got up and went outside. It had stopped raining, but even the sky looked wounded as the sun came up red and angry. For many, it would be a long, sad day.

Soon the children were up and playing around the house. Grandmother opened a tin of sardines— sardine tins were earthquake-proof, it seemed—while Mumtaz's wife made chapattis. They went quite well with the sardines. Pickle enjoyed them too.

Grandfather had washed and bandaged his head, and he was beginning to feel normal again.

'Will we be going away?' asked Rakesh, munching a sardine rolled up in chapatti.

'I suppose we'll have to,' said Grandmother. 'We can go to Calcutta, or stay with your father on the tea estates.'

'I don't want to go,' said Mukesh.

'Mukesh always wants to do the opposite of everyone else,' said Rakesh. 'What about you, Dolly? What do you want to do?'

'Dig up my doll's house,' said Dolly.

'We'll get you another,' said Rakesh. 'I'll make one for you.'

'It will have to be Calcutta,' said Grandfather. 'There are schools there. Lots of them.'

'No,' said Rakesh. 'We like it here. The school will start again.'

'But we don't have a house now!'

'We can build it again, can't we?'

'Yes,' agreed Mukesh. 'We can build it again!'

'Build it again,' repeated Dolly, 'build it again!'

'All easier said than done,' said Grandmother. 'But where's the money to come from?'

'What's our Daddy for?' Rakesh wanted to know.

'He has a job. He can send us money to build a new house, can't he? That's what fathers are for!'

'Yes, I suppose he could,' said Grandmother, opening another tin of sardines. 'That's what sons are for!'

Grandfather was standing at the gate when he saw his friend Azad, the carpenter, passing along the road, looking drawn and pale. Azad raised his hand in greeting and made as if to pass on; usually he stopped to talk.

'What's the hurry, Azad?' asked Grandfather. 'There's going to be enough work in town to keep you busy for more than a year.'

'But for what—for whom?' said Azad, without stopping. 'My wife and daughter are lying in the military hospital—it's the only one left—and I don't know if they will live . . . I'm sleeping there too, as my own house has gone.'

And there were others like him who had suffered greatly . . . Mumtaz brought home an eight-year-old girl, a distant cousin of his, who'd lost both her parents when the roofs of their houses fell in.

'How will she manage alone?' asked Grandmother.

'I'll look after her,' said Mumtaz. 'I wanted another daughter.'

'It won't be easy for you,' said Grandmother.

'You must let us help.'

'It is god's will,' said Mumtaz. 'He has spared us—we must care for those who were not so fortunate.'

* * *

While most of the survivors of the earthquake began leaving the town, Grandfather and his family began the task of putting their property together again. They would clear the rubble, salvage what could still be used, and then start from scratch; but Grandfather had decided to use only the smaller bricks together with light wooden frames. 'So that if there's another earthquake,' he said, 'we can sway and rock like Mumtaz's hut, instead of crashing to the ground.'

'I suppose there's something to be learnt from a disaster,' said Grandmother.

A neighbour looked over the broken wall and asked, 'Aren't you people leaving?'

'No,' said Grandfather. 'We're staying.'

'The experts say there's sure to be another earthquake.'

'Who knows?' said Grandfather.

'Don't you believe the experts?'

'Did they predict *this* earthquake?'

'No, they didn't,' admitted the neighbour.

'So why run away? Where are you off to?'

'Cuttack.'

'The expert's predict there'll be a cyclone in Cuttack.'

The neighbour threw up his arms in horror and walked away, looking thoughtful; perhaps Cuttack wasn't such a good idea after all. Where *did* one go, in order to escape disaster?

Grandfather and the family had decided to stay where they had always lived and face it out. Maybe there *would* be another earthquake. But they'd be prepared this time. And meanwhile, there were a few compensations. Mukesh and Dolly had recovered some of their toys and dolls, battered but still recognizable; Grandmother's oven had turned up almost intact from the bottom of the rubble, and biscuits were about to be made; and Grandfather had recovered his twisted tin bathtub and hammered it back into shape.

He'd placed it under the mango tree, filled it with hot water, and taken his bath in the afternoon sunshine. There hadn't been any soap, but there was plenty of mint in the garden. He started singing at the top of his voice, and the birds, who had just begun to return to the grove, took off in alarm and flew away again.

Riding through
the Flames

1

As Romi was about to mount his bicycle, he saw smoke rising from behind the distant line of trees.

'It looks like a forest fire,' said Prem, his friend and classmate.

'It's well to the east,' said Romi. 'Nowhere near the road.'

'There's a strong wind,' said Prem, looking at the dry leaves swirling across the road.

It was the middle of May, and it hadn't rained for several weeks. The grass was brown, the leaves of the trees covered with dust. Even though it was getting on to six o'clock in the evening, the boys' shirts were damp with sweat.

'It will be getting dark soon,' said Prem. 'You'd better spend the night at my house.'

'No, I said I'd be home tonight. My father isn't

keeping well. The doctor has given me some pills for him.'

'You'd better hurry, then. That fire seems to be spreading.'

'Oh, it's far off. It will take me only forty minutes to ride through the forest. Bye, Prem—see you tomorrow!'

Romi mounted his bicycle and pedalled off down the main road of the village, scattering stray hens, stray dogs and stray villagers.

'Hey, look where you're going!' shouted an angry villager, leaping out of the way of the oncoming bicycle. 'Do you think you own the road?'

'Of course I own it,' called Romi cheerfully, and cycled on.

His own village lay about seven miles distant, on the other side of the forest; but there was only a primary school in his village, and Romi was now at high school. His father, who was a fairly wealthy sugar cane farmer, had only recently bought him the bicycle. Romi didn't care too much for school and felt there weren't enough holidays but he enjoyed the long rides, and he got on well with "his classmates.

He might have stayed the night with Prem had

it not been for the pills which the vaid—the village doctor—had given him for his father. Romi's father was having back trouble, and the pills had been specially prepared from local herbs. Having been given such a fine bicycle, Romi felt that the least he could do in return was to get those pills to his father as early as possible. He put his head down and rode swiftly out of the village. Ahead of him, the smoke rose from the burning forest and the sky glowed red.

II

He had soon left the village far behind. There was a slight climb, and Romi had to push harder on the pedals to get over the rise. Once over the top, the road went winding down to the edge of the forest.

This was the part Romi enjoyed the most. He relaxed, stopped pedalling, and allowed the bicycle to glide gently down the slope. Soon the wind was rushing past him, blowing his hair about his face and making his shirt billow out behind him. He burst into a song.

A dog from the village ran beside him, barking furiously. Romi shouted to the dog, encouraging him in the race.

Then the road straightened out, and Romi began pedalling again.

The dog, seeing the forest ahead, turned back to the village. It was afraid of the forest.

The smoke was thicker now, and Romi caught the smell of burning timber. But ahead of him the road was clear. He rode on.

It was a rough, dusty road, cut straight through the forest. Tall trees grew on either side, cutting off the last of the daylight. But the spreading glow of the fire on the right lit up the road, and giant tree-shadows danced before the boy on the bicycle.

Usually the road was deserted. This evening it was alive with wild creatures fleeing from the forest fire. The first animal that Romi saw was a hare, leaping across the road in front of him. It was followed by several more hares. Then a band of monkeys streamed across, chattering excitedly.

They'll be safe on the other side, thought Romi. The fire won't cross the road.

But it was coming closer. And realizing this, Romi pedalled harder. In half an hour he should be out of the forest.

Suddenly, from the side of the road, several

pheasants rose in the air, and with a *whoosh*, flew low across the path, just in front of the oncoming bicycle. Taken by surprise, Romi fell off. When he picked himself up and began brushing his clothes, he saw that his knee was bleeding. It wasn't a deep cut, but he allowed it to bleed a little, took out his handkerchief and bandaged his knee. Then he mounted the bicycle again.

He rode a bit slower now, because birds and animals kept coming out of the bushes.

Not only pheasants but smaller birds too were streaming across the road—parrots, jungle crows, owls, magpies—and the air was filled with their cries.

Everyone's on the move, thought Romi. It must be a really big fire.

He could see the flames now, reaching out from behind the trees on his right, and he could hear the crackling as the dry leaves caught fire. The air was hot on his face. Leaves, still alight or turning to cinders, floated past.

A herd of deer crossed the road and Romi had to stop until they had passed. Then he mounted again and rode on; but now, for the first time, he was feeling afraid.

|||

From ahead came a faint clanging sound. It wasn't an animal sound, Romi was sure of that. A fire engine? There were no fire engines within fifty miles.

The clanging came nearer and Romi discovered that the noise came from a small boy who was running along the forest path, two milk cans clattering at his side.

'Teju!' called Romi, recognizing a boy from a neighbouring village. 'What are you doing out here?'

'Trying to get home, of course,' said Teju, panting along beside the bicycle.

'Jump on,' said Romi, stopping for him.

Teju was only eight or nine—a couple of years younger than Romi. He had come to deliver milk to some road-workers, but the workers had left at the first signs of the fire, and Teju was hurrying home with his cans still full of milk.

He got up on the crossbar of the bicycle, and Romi moved on again. He was quite used to carrying friends on the crossbar.

'Keep beating your milk cans,' said Romi. 'Like that, the animals will know we are coming. My bell doesn't make enough noise. I'm going to get a *horn* for my cycle!'

'I never knew there were so many animals in the jungle,' said Teju. 'I saw a python in the middle of the road. It stretched right across!'

'What did you do?'

'Just kept running and jumped right over it!'

Teju continued to chatter but Romi's thoughts were on the fire, which was much closer now. Flames shot up from the dry grass and ran up the trunks of trees and along the branches. Smoke billowed out above the forest.

Romi's eyes were smarting and his hair and eyebrows felt scorched. He was feeling tired but he couldn't stop now; he had to get beyond the range of the fire. Another ten or fifteen minutes of steady riding would get them to the small wooden bridge that spanned the little river separating the forest from the sugar cane fields.

Once across the river, they would be safe. The fire could not touch them on the other side because the forest ended at the river's edge. But could they get to the river in time?

IV

Clang, clang, clang went Teju's milk cans. But the sounds of the fire grew louder too.

A tall silk-cotton tree, its branches leaning across the road, had caught fire. They were almost beneath it when there was a crash and a burning branch fell to the ground a few yards in front of them.

The boys had to get off the bicycle and leave the road, forcing their way through a tangle of thorny bushes on the left, dragging and pushing at the bicycle and only returning to the road some distance ahead of the burning tree.

'We won't get out in time,' said Teju, back on the crossbar but feeling disheartened.

'Yes, we will,' said Romi, pedalling with all his might.

'The fire hasn't crossed the road as yet.'

Even as he spoke, he saw a small flame leap up from the grass on the left. It wouldn't be long before more sparks and burning leaves were blown across the road to kindle the grass on the other side.

'Oh, look!' exclaimed Romi, bringing the bicycle to a sudden stop.

'What's wrong now?' asked Teju, rubbing his sore eyes. And then, through the smoke, he saw what was stopping them.

An elephant was standing in the middle of the road.

Teju slipped off the crossbar, his cans rolling on the ground, bursting open and spilling their contents.

The elephant was about forty feet away. It moved about restlessly, its big ears flapping as it turned its head from side to side, wondering which way to go.

From far to the left, where the forest was still untouched, a herd of elephants moved towards the river. The leader of the herd raised his trunk and trumpeted a call. Hearing it, the elephant on the road raised its own trunk and trumpeted a reply. Then it shambled off into the forest, in the direction of the herd, leaving the way clear.

'Come, Teju, jump on!' urged Romi. 'We can't stay here much longer!'

V

Teju forgot about his milk cans and pulled himself up on the crossbar. Romi ran forward with the bicycle, to gain speed, and mounted swiftly. He kept as far as possible to the left of the road, trying to ignore the flames, the crackling, the smoke and the scorching heat.

It seemed that all the animals who could get away had done so. The exodus across the road had stopped.

'We won't stop again,' said Romi, gritting his teeth. 'Not even for an elephant!'

'We're nearly there!' said Teju. He was perking up again.

A jackal, overcome by the heat and smoke, lay in the middle of the path, either dead or unconscious. Romi did not stop. He swerved round the animal. Then he put all his strength into one final effort.

He covered the last hundred yards at top speed, and then they were out of the forest, freewheeling down the sloping road to the river.

'Look!' shouted Teju. 'The bridge is on fire!'

Burning embers had floated down on to the small wooden bridge and the dry, ancient timber had quickly caught fire. It was now burning fiercely.

Romi did not hesitate. He left the road, riding the bicycle over sand and pebbles. Then with a rush they went down the river bank and into the water.

The next thing they knew they were splashing around, trying to find each other in the darkness.

'Help!' cried Teju. 'I'm drowning!'

VI

'Don't be silly,' said Romi. 'The water isn't deep— it's only up to the knees. Come here and grab hold of me.'

Teju splashed across and grabbed Romi by the belt.

'The water's so cold,' he said, his teeth chattering.

'Do you want to go back and warm yourself?' asked Romi. 'Some people are never satisfied. Come on, help me get the bicycle up. It's down here, just where we are standing.'

Together they managed to heave the bicycle out of the water and stand it upright.

'Now sit on it,' said Romi. 'I'll push you across.'

'We'll be swept away,' said Teju.

'No, we won't. There's not much water in the river at this time of the year. But the current is quite strong in the middle, so sit still. All right?'

'All right,' said Teju nervously.

Romi began guiding the bicycle across the river, one hand on the seat and one hand on the handlebar. The river was shallow and sluggish in midsummer; even so, it was quite swift in the middle. But having got safely out of the burning forest, Romi was in no mood to let a little river defeat him.

He kicked off his shoes, knowing they would be lost, and then gripping the smooth stones of the river bed with his toes, he concentrated on keeping his balance and getting the bicycle and Teju through the middle of the stream. The water here came up to his waist, and the current would have been too strong for Teju. But when they reached the shallows, Teju got down and helped Romi push the bicycle.

They reached the opposite bank and sank down on the grass.

'We can rest now,' said Romi. 'But not all night— I've got some medicine to give my father.' He felt in his pockets and found that the pills, in their envelope, had turned to a soggy mess. 'Oh well, he has to take them with water anyway,' he said.

They watched the fire as it continued to spread through the forest. It had crossed the road down which they had come. The sky was a bright red, and the river reflected the colour of the sky.

Several elephants had found their way down to the river. They were cooling off by spraying water on each other with their trunks. Further downstream there were deer and other animals.

Romi and Teju looked at each other in the glow from the fire. They hadn't known each other very well before. But now they felt they had been friends for years.

'What are you thinking about?' asked Teju.

'I'm thinking,' said Romi, 'that even if the fire is

out in a day or two, it will be a long time before the bridge is repaired. So I'm thinking it will be a nice long holiday from school!'

'But you can walk across the river,' said Teju. 'You just did it.'

'Impossible,' said Romi. 'It's much too swift.'

A Flight of Pigeons
(An Extract)

1

The revolt broke out at Meerut on the 10th of May, at the beginning of a very hot and oppressive summer. The sepoys shot down their English officers; there was rioting and looting in the city; the jail was broken open and armed convicts descended on English families living in the city and cantonment, setting fire to houses and killing the inmates. Several mutinous regiments marched to Delhi, their principal rallying point, where the peaceable, poetry-loving Emperor Bahadur Shah suddenly found himself the figurehead of the revolt.

The British Army, which had been cooling off in Shimla, began its long march to Delhi. But meanwhile, the conflict had spread to other cities. And on the 30th of May there was much excitement in the magistrate's office at Shahjahanpur, some 250 miles east of Delhi.

A bungalow in the cantonment, owned by the Redmans, an Anglo-Indian family, had been set on fire during the night. The Redmans had been able to escape, but most of their property was looted or destroyed. A familiar figure had been seen flitting around the grounds that night; and Javed Khan, a Rohilla Pathan, well known to everyone in the city, was arrested on suspicion of arson and brought before the magistrate.

* * *

The burning of the Redmans' bungalow failed to alert the small English community in Shahjahanpur to a sense of danger. Meerut was far away, and the *Moffusilite*, the local news sheet, carried very little news of the disturbances. The army officers made their rounds without noticing anything unusual, and the civilians went to their offices. In the evening they met in the usual fashion, to eat and drink and dance.

On the 30th of May it was Dr Bowling's turn as host. In his drawing room, young Lieutenant Scott strummed a guitar, while Mrs Bowling sang a romantic ballad. Four army officers sat down to a game of whist, while Mrs Ricketts, Mr Jenkins, the Collector, and Captain James discussed the weather over a bottle of Exshaw's whisky.

Only the Labadoors had any foreboding of trouble. They were not at the party.

Mr Labadoor was forty-two, his wife thirty-eight. Their daughter, Ruth, was a pretty girl, with raven black hair and dark, lustrous eyes. She had left Mrs Shield's school at Fatehgarh only a fortnight before, because her mother felt she would be safer at home.

Mrs Labadoor's father had been a French adventurer who had served in the Maratha army; her mother came from a well-known Muslim family of Rampur. Her name was Mariam. She and her brothers had been brought up as Christians. At eighteen, she married Labadoor, a quiet, unassuming man, who was a clerk in the magistrate's office. He was the grandson of a merchant from Jersey (in the Channel Islands), and his original Jersey name was Labadu.

While most of the British wives in the cantonment thought it beneath their dignity to gossip with servants, Mariam Labadoor, who made few social calls, enjoyed these conversations of hers. Often they enlivened her day by reporting the juiciest scandals, on which they were always well informed. But from what Mariam had heard recently, she was convinced that it was only a matter of hours before rioting broke out in the city. News of the events at Meerut had reached the bazaars and sepoy lines, and a fakir, who lived near the River Khannaut, was said to have predicted the end of the English East India Company's rule in the coming months. Mariam made her husband and daughter stay at home the evening of the Bowling's party, and had even suggested that they avoid going to church the next day, Sunday: a surprising request from Mariam, a regular church-goer.

Ruth liked having her way, and insisted on going to church the next day; and her father promised to accompany her.

* * *

The sun rose in a cloudless, shimmering sky, and only those who had risen at dawn had been lucky enough to enjoy the cool breeze that had blown across the river for a brief spell. At seven o'clock the church bell began to toll, and people could be seen making their way towards the small, sturdily built cantonment church. Some, like Mr Labadoor and his daughter, were on foot, wearing their Sunday clothes. Others came in carriages, or were borne aloft in *dolies* manned by sweating *dolie*-bearers.

St Mary's, the little church in Shahjahanpur, was situated on the southern boundary of the cantonment, near an ancient mango grove. There were three entrances: one to the south, facing a large compound known as Buller's; another to the west, below the steeple; and the vestry door opening to the north. A narrow staircase led up to the steeple. To the east there were open fields sloping down to the river, cultivated with melon; to the west lay an open plain bounded by the city; while the parade ground stretched away to the north until it reached the barracks of the sepoys. The bungalows scattered about the side of the parade ground belonged to the regimental officers, Englishmen who had slept soundly, quite unaware of an atmosphere charged with violence.

I will let Ruth take up the story . . .

At the Church

Father and I had just left the house when we saw several sepoys crossing the road, on their way to the river for their morning bath. They stared so fiercely at us that I pressed close to my father and whispered, 'Papa, how strange they look!' But their appearance did not strike him as unusual: the sepoys usually passed that way when going to the River Khannaut, and I suppose Father was used to meeting them on his way to office.

We entered the church from the south porch, and took our seats in the last pew to the right. A number of people had already arrived, but I did not particularly notice who they were. We had knelt down, and were in the middle of the Confession, when we heard a tumult outside and a lot of shouting that seemed nearer every moment. Everyone in the church got up, and Father left our pew and went and stood at the door, where I joined him.

There were six or seven men on the porch. Their faces were covered up to their noses, and they wore tight loincloths as though they had prepared for a wrestling bout; but they held naked swords in their hands. As soon as they saw us, they sprang forward, and one of them made a cut at us. The sword missed us both and caught the side of the door where it buried itself in the wood. My father had his left hand against the door, and I rushed out from under it, and escaped into the church compound.

A second and third cut were made at my father by the others, both of which caught him on his right cheek. Father tried to seize the sword of one of his assailants, but he caught it high up on the blade, and so firmly that he lost two fingers from his right hand. These were the only cuts he received; but though he did not fall, he was bleeding profusely. All this time I had stood looking on from the porch, completely bewildered and dazed by what had happened. I remember asking my father what had happened to make him bleed so much.

'Take the handkerchief from my pocket and bandage my face,' he said.

When I had made a bandage from both our handkerchiefs and tied it about his head, he said he wished to go home. I took him by the hand and tried to lead him out of the porch; but we had gone only a few steps when he began to feel faint, and said, 'I can't walk, Ruth. Let us go back to the church.'

* * *

The armed men had made only one rush through the church, and had then gone off through the vestry door. After wounding my father, they had run up the centre of the aisle, slashing right and left. They had taken a cut at Lieutenant Scott, but his mother threw herself over him and received the blow on her ribs; her tight clothes saved her from a serious injury. Mr Ricketts, Mr Jenkins, the Collector, and Mr MacCullam, the minister, ran out through the vestry.

The rest of the congregation had climbed up to the belfry, and on my father's urging me to do so, I joined them there. We saw Captain James riding up to the church, quite unaware of what was happening. We shouted him a warning, but as he looked up at us, one of the sepoys, who were scattered about on the parade ground, fired at him, and he fell from his horse. Now two other officers came running from the Mess, calling out to the sepoys: 'Oh! children, what are you doing?' They tried to pacify their men, but no one listened to them. They had, however, been popular officers with the sepoys, who did not prevent them from joining us in the turret with their pistols in their hands.

Just then we saw a carriage coming at full speed towards the church. It was Dr Bowling's, and it carried him, his wife and child, and the nanny. The carriage had to cross the parade ground, and they were halfway across when a bullet hit the doctor who was sitting on the coach box. He doubled up in his seat, but did not let go of the reins, and the carriage had almost reached the church, when a sepoy ran up and made a slash at Mrs Bowling, missing her by inches. When the carriage reached the church, some of the officers ran down to help Dr Bowling off the coach box. He struggled in their arms for a while, and was dead when they got him to the ground.

I had come down from the turret with the officers, and now ran to where my father lay. He was sitting against the wall, in a large pool of blood. He did not complain of any pain, but his lips were parched, and he kept his eyes open with an effort. He told me to go home, and to ask Mother to send someone with a cot, or a *dolie*, to carry him back. So much had happened so quickly that I was completely dazed, and though Mrs Bowling and the other women were weeping, there wasn't a tear in my eye. There were two great wounds on my father's face, and I was reluctant to leave him, but to run home and fetch a *dolie* seemed to be the only way in which I could help him.

Leaving him against the stone wall of the church, I ran round to the vestry side and almost fell over Mr Ricketts, who was lying about twelve feet from the vestry door. He had been attacked by an expert and powerful swordsman, whose blow had cut through the trunk from the left shoulder, separating the head and right hand from the rest of the body. Sick with horror, I turned from the spot and began running home through Buller's compound.

Nobody met me on the way. No one challenged me, or tried to intercept or molest me. The cantonment seemed empty and deserted; but just as I reached the end of Buller's compound, I saw our house in flames. I stopped at the gate, looking about for my mother, but could not see her anywhere. Granny, too, was missing, and the servants. Then I saw Lala Ramjimal walking down the road towards me.

'Don't worry, my child,' he said. 'Mother, Granny and the others are all safe. Come, I will take you to them.'

There was no question of doubting Lala Ramjimal's intentions. He had held me on his knee when I was a baby, and I had grown up under his eyes. He led me to a hut some thirty yards from our old home. It was a mud house, facing the road, and its door was closed. Lala knocked on the door, but received no answer; then he put his mouth to a chink and whispered, '*Missy-baba* is with me, open the door.'

The door opened, and I rushed into my mother's arms.

'Thank god!' she cried. 'At least one is spared to me.'

'Papa is wounded at the church,' I said. 'Send someone to fetch him.'

Mother looked up at Lala and he could not resist the appeal in her eyes.

'I will go,' he said. 'Do not move from here until I return.'

'You don't know where he is,' I said. 'Let me come with you and help you.'

'No, you must not leave your mother now,' said Lala. 'If you are seen with me, we shall both be killed.'

He returned in the afternoon, after several hours. 'Sahib is dead,' he said, very simply. 'I arrived in time to see him die. He had lost so much blood that it was impossible for him to live. He could not speak and his eyes were becoming glazed, but he looked at me in such a way that I am sure he recognized me . . .'

Lala Ramjimal

Lala left us in the afternoon, promising to return when it grew dark, then he would take us to his own house. He ran a grave risk in doing so, but he had promised us his protection, and he was a man who once he had decided on taking a certain course of action, could not be shaken from his purpose. He was not a Government servant and owed no loyalties to the British; nor had he conspired with the rebels for his path never crossed theirs. He had been content always to go about his business (he owned several *dolies* and carriages, which he hired out to the Europeans who could not buy their own) in a quiet and efficient manner, and was held in some respect by those he came into contact with; his motives were always personal and if he helped us, it was not because we belonged to the ruling class—my father was probably the most junior officer in Shahjahanpur—but because he had known us for many years, and had grown fond of my mother, who had always treated him as a friend and equal.

I realized that I was now fatherless, and my mother, a widow; but we had no time to indulge in our private sorrow. Our own lives were in constant danger. From our hiding place we could hear the crackling of timber coming from our burning house. The road from the city to the cantonment was in an uproar, with people shouting on all sides. We heard the tramp of men passing up and down the road, just in front of our door; a moan or a sneeze would have betrayed us, and then we would have been at the mercy of the most ruffianly elements from the bazaar, whose swords flashed in the dazzling sunlight.

There were eight of us in the little room: Mother, Granny, myself; my cousin, Anet; my mother's half-brother, Pilloo, who was about my age, and his mother; our servants, Champa and Lado; as well as two of our black-and-white spaniels, who had followed close on Mother's heels when she fled from the house.

The mud hut in which we were sheltering was

owned by Tirloki, a mason who had helped build our own house. He was well known to us. Weeks before the outbreak, when Mother used to gossip with her servants and others about the possibility of trouble in Shahjahanpur, Tirloki had been one of those who had offered his house for shelter should she ever be in need of it. And Mother, as a precaution, had accepted his offer, and taken the key from him.

Mother afterwards told me that as she sat on the veranda that morning, one of the gardener's sons had come running to her in great haste and had cried out: 'Mutiny broken out, sahib and *missy-baba* killed!' Hearing that we had both been killed, Mother's first impulse was to throw herself into the nearest well; but Granny caught hold of her, and begged her not to be rash, saying, 'And what will become of the rest of us if you do such a thing?' And so she had gone across the road, followed by the others, and had entered Tirloki's house and chained the door from within.

* * *

We were shut up in the hut all day, expecting, at any moment, to be discovered and killed. We had no food at all, but we could not have eaten any had it been there. My father gone, our future appeared a perfect void, and we found it difficult to talk. A hot wind blew through the cracks in the door, and our throats were parched. Late in the afternoon, a *chatty* of cold water was let down to us from a tree outside a window at the rear of the hut. This was an act of compassion on the part of a man called Chinta, who had worked for us as a labourer when our bungalow was being built.

At about ten o'clock, Lala returned, accompanied by Dhani, our old bearer. He proposed to take us to his own house. Mother hesitated to come out into the open, but Lala assured her that the roads were quite clear now, and there was little fear of our being molested. At last, she agreed to go.

We formed two batches. Lala led the way with a drawn sword in one hand, his umbrella in the other. Mother and Anet and I followed, holding each other's hands. Mother had thrown over us a counterpane which she had been carrying with her when she left the house. We avoided the main road, making our way round the sweeper settlement, and reached Lala's house after a fifteen-minute walk. On our arrival there, Lala offered us a bed to sit upon, while he squatted down on the ground with his legs crossed.

Mother had thrown away her big bunch of keys as we left Tirloki's house. When I asked her why she had done so, she pointed to the smouldering ruins of our bungalow and said: 'Of what possible use could they be to us now?'

The bearer, Dhani, arrived with the second batch, consisting of dear Granny, Pilloo and his mother, and Champa and Lado, and the dogs. There were eight of us in Lala's small house; and, as far as I could tell, his own family was as large as ours.

We were offered food, but we could not eat. We lay down for the night—Mother, Granny and I on the bed, the rest on the ground. And in the darkness, with my face against my mother's bosom, I gave vent to my grief and wept bitterly. My mother wept, too, but silently, and I think she was still weeping when at last I fell asleep.

In Lala's House

Lala Ramjimal's family consisted of himself, his wife, mother, aunt and sister. It was a house of women, and our unexpected arrival hadn't changed that. It must indeed have been a test of the Lala's strength and patience, with twelve near-hysterical females on his hands!

His family, of course, knew who we were, because

Lala's mother and aunt used to come and draw water from our well, and offer bel leaves at the little shrine near our house. They were at first shy of us; and we, so immersed in our own predicament, herded together in a corner of the house, looked at each other's faces and wept. Lala's wife would come and serve us food in platters made of stitched leaves. We ate once in twenty-four hours, a little after noon, but we were satisfied with this one big meal.

The house was an ordinary mud building, consisting of four flat-roofed rooms, with a low veranda in the front, and a courtyard at the back. It was small and unpretentious, occupied by a family of small means.

Lala's wife was a young woman, short in stature, with a fair complexion. We didn't know her name, because it is not customary for a husband or wife to call the other by name; but her mother-in-law would address her as *dulhan*, or bride.

Ramjimal himself was a tall, lean man, with a long moustache. His speech was always very polite, like that of most Kayasthas but he had an air of determination about him that was rare in others.

On the second day of our arrival, I overheard his mother speaking to him: 'Lalaji, you have made a great mistake in bringing these *Angrezans* into our house. What will people say? As soon as the rebels hear of it, they will come and kill us.'

'I have done what is right,' replied Lala very quietly. 'I have not given shelter to *Angrezans*. I have given shelter to friends. Let people say or think as they please.'

He seldom went out of the house, and was usually to be seen seated before the front door, either smoking his small hookah, or playing chess with some friend, who happened to drop by. After a few days, people began to suspect that there was somebody in the house about whom Lala was being very discreet, but they had no idea who these guests could be. He kept a close watch on his family, to prevent them from talking too much; and he saw that no one entered the house, keeping the front door chained at all times.

It is a wonder that we were able to live undiscovered for as long as we did, for there were always the dogs to draw attention to the house. They would not leave us, though we had nothing to offer them except the leftovers from our own meals. Lala's aunt told Mother that the third of our dogs, who had not followed us, had been seen going round and round the smoking ruins of our bungalow, and that on the day after the outbreak, he was found dead, sitting up—waiting for his master's return!

Escape from Java

It all happened within the space of a few days. The cassia tree had barely come into flower when the first bombs fell on Batavia (now called Jakarta) and the bright pink blossoms lay scattered over the wreckage in the streets.

News had reached us that Singapore had fallen to the Japanese. My father said, 'I expect it won't be long before they take Java. With the British defeated, how can the Dutch be expected to win!' He did not mean to be critical of the Dutch; he knew they did not have the backing of the Empire that Britain had. Singapore had been called the Gibraltar of the East. After its surrender there could only be retreat, a vast exodus of Europeans from South-East Asia.

It was the Second World War. What the Javanese thought about the war is now hard for me to say, because I was only nine at the time and knew very little of worldly matters. Most people knew they would be exchanging their Dutch rulers for Japanese rulers; but there were also many who spoke in terms of freedom for Java when the war was over.

Our neighbour, Mr Hartono, was one of those who looked ahead to a time when Java, Sumatra and the other islands would make up one independent nation. He was a college professor and spoke Dutch, Chinese, Javanese and a little English. His son, Sono, was about my age. He was the only boy I knew who could talk to me in English, and as a result we spent a lot of time together. Our favourite pastime was flying kites in the park.

The bombing soon put an end to kite flying. Air raid alerts sounded at all hours of the day and night and, although in the beginning most of the bombs fell near the docks, a couple of miles from where we lived, we had to stay indoors. If the planes sounded very near, we dived under beds or tables. I don't remember if there were any trenches. Probably there hadn't been time for trench digging, and now there was time only for digging graves. Events had moved all too swiftly, and everyone (except, of course, the Javanese) was anxious to get away from Java.

'When are you going?' asked Sono, as we sat on the veranda steps in a pause between air raids.

'I don't know,' I said. 'It all depends on my father.'

'My father says the Japs will be here in a week. And if you're still here then, they'll put you to work building a railway.'

'I wouldn't mind building a railway,' I said.

'But they won't give you enough to eat. Just rice with worms in it. And if you don't work properly, they'll shoot you.'

'They do that to soldiers,' I said. 'We're civilians.'

'They do it to civilians, too,' said Sono.

What were my father and I doing in Batavia, when our home had been first in India and then in Singapore? He worked for a firm dealing in rubber, and six months earlier he had been sent to Batavia to open a new office in partnership with a Dutch business house. Although I was so young, I accompanied my father almost everywhere. My mother left when I was very small, and my father had always looked after me. After the war was over he was going to take me to England.

'Are we going to win the war?' I asked.

'It doesn't look it from here,' he said.

No, it didn't look as though we were winning. Standing at the docks with my father, I watched the ships arrive from Singapore crowded with refugees—

men, women and children, all living on the decks in the hot tropical sun; they looked pale and worn out and worried. They were on their way to Colombo or Bombay. No one came ashore at Batavia. It wasn't British territory; it was Dutch, and everyone knew it wouldn't be Dutch for long.

'Aren't we going too?' I asked. 'Sono's father says the Japs will be here any day.'

'We've still got a few days,' said my father. He was a short, stocky man who seldom got excited. If he was worried, he didn't show it. 'I've got to wind up a few business matters, and then we'll be off.'

'How will we go? There's no room for us on those ships.'

'There certainly isn't. But we'll find a way, lad, don't worry.'

I didn't worry. I had complete confidence in my father's ability to find a way out of difficulties. He used to say, 'Every problem has a solution hidden away somewhere, and if only you look hard enough you will find it.'

There were British soldiers in the streets but they did not make it feel much safer. They were just waiting for troop ships to come and take them away.

No one, it seemed, was interested in defending Java, only in getting out as fast as possible.

Although the Dutch were unpopular with the Javanese people, there was no ill feeling against individual Europeans. I could walk safely through the streets. Occasionally small boys in the crowded Chinese quarter would point at me and shout, 'Orang Balandi!' (Dutchman!) but they did so in good humour, and I didn't know the language well enough to stop and explain that the English weren't Dutch. For them, all white people were the same, and understandably so.

My father's office was in the commercial area, along the canal banks. Our two-storied house, about a mile away, was an old building with a roof of red tiles and a broad balcony which had stone dragons at either end. There were flowers in the garden almost all the year round. If there was anything in Batavia more regular than the bombing, it was the rain, which came pattering down on the roof and on the banana fronds almost every afternoon. In the hot and steamy atmosphere of Java, the rain was always welcome.

There were no anti-aircraft guns in Batavia—at

least we never heard any—and the Jap bombers came over at will, dropping their bombs by daylight. Sometimes bombs fell in the town. One day the building next to my father's office received a direct hit and tumbled into the river. A number of office workers were killed.

The schools closed, and Sono and I had nothing to do all day except sit in the house, playing darts or carrom, wrestling on the carpets, or playing the gramophone. We had records by Gracie Fields, Harry Lauder, George Formby and Arthur Askey, all popular British artists of the early 1940s. One song by Arthur Askey made fun of Adolph Hitler, with the words, 'Adolph, we're gonna hang up your washing on the Siegfried Line, if the Siegfried Line's still there!' It made us feel quite cheerful to know that back in Britain people were confident of winning the war!

One day Sono said, 'The bombs are falling on Batavia, not in the countryside. Why don't we get cycles and ride out of town?'

I fell in with the idea at once. After the morning all-clear had sounded, we mounted our cycles and rode out of town. Mine was a hired cycle, but Sono's was his own. He'd had it since the age of five, and it was constantly in need of repair. 'The soul has gone out of it,' he used to say.

Our fathers were at work; Sono's mother had gone out to do her shopping (during air raids she took shelter under the most convenient shop counter) and wouldn't be back for at least an hour. We expected to be back before lunch.

We were soon out of town, on a road that passed through rice fields, pineapple orchards and cinchona plantations. On our right lay dark green hills; on our left, groves of coconut palms and, beyond them, the sea. Men and women were working in the rice fields, knee-deep in mud, their broad-brimmed hats protecting them from the fierce sun. Here and there a buffalo wallowed in a pool of brown water, while a naked boy lay stretched out on the animal's broad back.

We took a bumpy track through the palms. They grew right down to the edge of the sea. Leaving our cycles on the shingle, we ran down a smooth, sandy beach and into the shallow water.

'Don't go too far in,' warned Sono. 'There may be sharks about.'

Wading in amongst the rocks, we searched for interesting shells, then sat down on a large rock and looked out to sea, where a sailing ship moved placidly on the crisp, blue waters. It was difficult to imagine that half the world was at war, and that Batavia, two or three miles away, was right in the middle of it.

On our way home we decided to take a short cut through the rice fields, but soon found that our tyres got bogged down in the soft mud. This delayed our return; and to make things worse, we got the roads mixed up and reached an area of the town that seemed unfamiliar. We had barely entered the outskirts when the siren sounded, followed soon after by the drone of approaching aircraft.

'Should we get off our cycles and take shelter somewhere?' I called out.

'No, let's race home!' shouted Sono. 'The bombs won't fall here.'

But he was wrong. The planes flew in very low. Looking up for a moment, I saw the sun blotted out by the sinister shape of a Jap fighter-bomber. We pedalled furiously; but we had barely covered fifty yards when there was a terrific explosion on our right, behind some houses. The shock sent us spinning across the road. We were flung from our cycles. And the cycles, still propelled by the blast, crashed into a wall.

I felt a stinging sensation in my hands and legs, as though scores of little insects had bitten me. Tiny droplets of blood appeared here and there on my flesh. Sono was on all fours, crawling beside me, and I saw that he too had the same small scratches on his hands and forehead, made by tiny shards of flying glass.

We were quickly on our feet, and then we began running in the general direction of our homes. The twisted cycles lay forgotten on the road.

'Get off the street, you two!' shouted someone from a window; but we weren't going to stop running until we got home. And we ran faster than we'd ever run in our lives.

My father and Sono's parents were themselves running about the street, calling for us, when we came rushing around the corner and tumbled into their arms.

'Where have you been?'

'What happened to you?'

'How did you get those cuts?'

All superfluous questions but before we could recover our breath and start explaining, we were bundled into our respective homes. My father washed my cuts and scratches, dabbed at my face and legs with iodine—ignoring my yelps—and then stuck plaster all over my face.

Sono and I had had a fright, and we did not venture far from the house again.

That night my father said: 'I think we'll be able to leave in a day or two.'

'Has another ship come in?'

'No.'

'Then how are we going? By plane?'

'Wait and see, lad. It isn't settled yet. But we won't be able to take much with us—just enough to fill a couple of travelling bags.'

'What about the stamp collection?' I asked.

My father's stamp collection was quite valuable and filled several volumes.

'I'm afraid we'll have to leave most of it behind,' he said. 'Perhaps Mr Hartono will keep it for me, and when the war is over—if it's over—we'll come back for it.'

'But we can take one or two albums with us, can't we?'

'I'll take one. There'll be room for one. Then if we're short of money in Bombay, we can sell the stamps.'

'Bombay? That's in India. I thought we were going back to England.'

'First we must go to India.'

The following morning I found Sono in the garden, patched up like me, and with one foot in a bandage. But he was as cheerful as ever and gave me his usual wide grin.

'We're leaving tomorrow,' I said.

The grin left his face.

'I will be sad when you go,' he said. 'But I will be glad too, because then you will be able to escape from the Japs.'

'After the war, I'll come back.'

'Yes, you must come back. And then, when we are big, we will go round the world together. I want to see England and America and Africa and India and Japan. I want to go everywhere.'

'We can't go everywhere.'

'Yes, we can. No one can stop us!'

We had to be up very early the next morning. Our bags had been packed late at night. We were taking a few clothes, some of my father's business papers, a pair of binoculars, one stamp album, and several bars of chocolate. I was pleased about the stamp album and the chocolates, but I had to give up several of my treasures—favourite books, the gramophone and records, an old Samurai sword, a train set and a dartboard. The only consolation was that Sono, and not a stranger, would have them.

In the first faint light of dawn a truck drew up in front of the house. It was driven by a Dutch businessman, Mr Hookens, who worked with my father. Sono was already at the gate, waiting to say goodbye.

'I have a present for you,' he said.

He took me by the hand and pressed a smooth hard object into my palm. I grasped it and then held it up against the light. It was a beautiful little sea horse, carved out of pale blue jade.

'It will bring you luck,' said Sono.

'Thank you,' I said. 'I will keep it forever.'

And I slipped the little sea horse into my pocket.

'In you get, lad,' said my father, and I got up on the front seat between him and Mr Hookens.

As the truck started up, I turned to wave to Sono. He was sitting on his garden wall, grinning at me. He called out: 'We will go everywhere, and no one can stop us!'

He was still waving when the truck took us round the bend at the end of the road.

We drove through the still, quiet streets of Batavia, occasionally passing burnt-out trucks and shattered buildings. Then we left the sleeping city far behind and were climbing into the forested hills. It had rained during the night, and when the sun came up over the green hills, it twinkled and glittered on the broad, wet leaves. The light in the forest changed from dark green to greenish gold, broken here and there by the flaming red or orange of a trumpet-shaped blossom. It was impossible to know the names of all those fantastic plants! The road had been cut through a dense tropical forest, and on either side the trees jostled each other, hungry for the sun; but they were chained together by the liana creepers and vines that fed upon the struggling trees.

Occasionally a jelarang, a large Javan squirrel, frightened by the passing of the truck, leapt through the trees before disappearing into the depths of the forest. We saw many birds: peacocks, junglefowl, and once, standing majestically at the side of the road, a crowned pigeon, its great size and splendid crest making it a striking object even at a distance. Mr Hookens slowed down so that we could look at the bird. It bowed its head so that its crest swept the ground; then it emitted a low hollow boom rather than the call of a turkey.

When we came to a small clearing, we stopped for breakfast. Butterflies, black, green and gold, flitted across the clearing. The silence of the forest was broken only by the drone of airplanes. Japanese Zeros heading for Batavia on another raid. I thought about Sono, and wondered what he would be doing at home: probably trying out the gramophone!

We ate boiled eggs and drank tea from a thermos, then got back into the truck and resumed our journey.

I must have dozed off soon after, because the next thing I remember is that we were going quite fast down a steep, winding road, and in the distance I could see a calm blue lagoon.

'We've reached the sea again,' I said.

'That's right,' said my father. 'But we're now nearly a hundred miles from Batavia, in another part of the island. You're looking out over the Sunda Straits.'

Then he pointed towards a shimmering white object resting on the waters of the lagoon.

'There's our plane,' he said.

'A seaplane!' I exclaimed. 'I never guessed. Where will it take us?'

'To Bombay, I hope. There aren't many other places left to go to!'

It was a very old seaplane, and no one, not even the captain—the pilot was called the captain—could promise that it would take off. Mr Hookens wasn't coming with us; he said the plane would be back for him the next day. Besides my father and me, there were four other passengers, and all but one were Dutch. The odd man out was a Londoner, a motor mechanic who'd been left behind in Java when his unit was evacuated. (He told us later that he'd fallen asleep at a bar in the Chinese quarter, waking up some hours after his regiment had moved off!) He looked rather scruffy. He'd lost the top button of his shirt, but, instead of leaving his collar open, as we did, he'd kept it together with a large safety pin, which thrust itself out from behind a bright pink tie.

'It's a relief to find you here, guvnor,' he said, shaking my father by the hand. 'Knew you for a Yorkshireman the minute I set eyes on you. It's the songfried that does it, if you know what I mean.' (He meant sangfroid, French for a 'cool look'.) 'And here I was, with all these flippin' forriners, and me not knowing a word of what they've been yattering about. Do you think this old tub will get us back to Blighty?'

'It does look a bit shaky,' said my father. 'One of the first flying boats, from the looks of it. If it gets us to Bombay, that's far enough.'

'Anywhere out of Java's good enough for me,' said our new companion. 'The name's Muggeridge.'

'Pleased to know you, Mr Muggeridge,' said my father. 'I'm Bond. This is my son.'

Mr Muggeridge rumpled my hair and favoured me with a large wink.

The captain of the seaplane was beckoning to us to join him in a small skiff which was about to take us across a short stretch of water to the seaplane.

'Here we go,' said Mr Muggeridge. 'Say your prayers and keep your fingers crossed.'

The seaplane was a long time getting airborne. It had to make several runs before it finally took off. Then, lurching drunkenly, it rose into the clear blue sky.

'For a moment I thought we were going to end up in the briny,' said Mr Muggeridge, untying his seat belt. 'And talkin' of fish, I'd give a week's wages for a plate of fish an' chips and a pint of beer.'

'I'll buy you a beer in Bombay,' said my father.

'Have an egg,' I said, remembering we still had some boiled eggs in one of the travelling bags.

'Thanks, mate,' said Mr Muggeridge, accepting an egg with alacrity. 'A real egg, too! I've been livin' on egg powder these last six months. That's what they give you in the army. And it ain't hens' eggs they make it from, let me tell you. It's either gulls' or turtles' eggs!'

'No,' said my father with a straight face. 'Snakes' eggs.'

Mr Muggeridge turned a delicate shade of green; but he soon recovered his poise, and for about an hour kept talking about almost everything under the sun, including Churchill, Hitler, Roosevelt, Mahatma Gandhi, and Betty Grable. (The last-named was famous for her beautiful legs.) He would have gone on talking all the way to Bombay had he been given a chance, but suddenly a shudder passed through the old plane, and it began lurching again.

'I think an engine is giving trouble,' said my father.

When I looked through the small glassed-in window, it seemed as though the sea was rushing up to meet us.

The co-pilot entered the passenger cabin and said something in Dutch. The passengers looked dismayed, and immediately began fastening their seat belts.

'Well, what did the blighter say?' asked Mr Muggeridge.

'I think he's going to have to ditch the plane,' said my father, who knew enough Dutch to get the gist of anything that was said.

'Down in the drink!' exclaimed Mr Muggeridge.

'Gawd 'elp us! And how far are we from Bombay, guv?'

'A few hundred miles,' said my father.

'Can you swim, mate?' asked Mr Muggeridge looking at me.

'Yes,' I said. 'But not all the way to Bombay. How far can you swim?'

'The length of a bathtub,' he said.

'Don't worry,' said my father. 'Just make sure your life jacket's properly tied.'

We looked to our life jackets; my father checked mine twice, making sure that it was properly fastened.

The pilot had now cut both engines, and was bringing the plane down in a circling movement. But he couldn't control the speed, and it was tilting heavily to one side. Instead of landing smoothly on its belly, it came down on a wing tip, and this caused the plane to swivel violently around in the choppy sea. There was a terrific jolt when the plane hit the water, and if it hadn't been for the seat belts we'd have been flung from our seats. Even so, Mr Muggeridge struck his head against the seat in front, and he was now holding a bleeding nose and using some shocking language.

As soon as the plane came to a standstill, my father undid my seat belt. There was no time to lose. Water was already filling the cabin, and all the passengers—except one, who was dead in his seat with a broken neck—were scrambling for the exit hatch. The co-pilot pulled a lever and the door fell away to reveal high waves slapping against the sides of the stricken plane.

Holding me by the hand, my father was leading me towards the exit.

'Quick, lad,' he said. 'We won't stay afloat for long.'

'Give us a hand!' shouted Mr Muggeridge, still struggling with his life jacket. 'First this bloody bleedin' nose, and now something's gone and stuck.'

My father helped him fix the life jacket, then pushed him out of the door ahead of us.

As we swam away from the seaplane (Mr Muggeridge splashing fiercely alongside us), we were aware of the other passengers in the water. One of them shouted to us in Dutch to follow him.

We swam after him towards the dinghy, which had been released the moment we hit the water. That yellow dinghy, bobbing about on the waves, was as welcome as land.

All who had left the plane managed to climb into the dinghy. We were seven altogether—a tight fit. We had hardly settled down in the well of the dinghy when Mr Muggeridge, still holding his nose, exclaimed:—'There she goes!' And as we looked on helplessly, the seaplane sank swiftly and silently beneath the waves.

The dinghy had shipped a lot of water, and soon everyone was busy bailing it out with mugs (there were a couple in the dinghy), hats, and bare hands. There was a light swell, and every now and then water would roll in again and half fill the dinghy. But within half an hour we had most of the water out, and then it was possible to take turns, two men doing the bailing while the others rested. No one expected me to do this work, but I gave a hand anyway, using my father's sola topi for the purpose.

'Where are we?' asked one of the passengers.

'A long way from anywhere,' said another.

'There must be a few islands in the Indian Ocean.'

'But we may be at sea for days before we come to one of them.'

'Days or even weeks,' said the captain. 'Let us look at our supplies.'

The dinghy appeared to be fairly well provided with emergency rations: biscuits, raisins, chocolates (we'd lost our own), and enough water to last a week. There was also a first-aid box, which was put to immediate use, as Mr Muggeridge's nose needed attention. A few others had cuts and bruises. One of the passengers had received a hard knock on the head and appeared to be suffering from a loss of memory. He had no idea how we happened to be drifting about in the middle of the Indian Ocean; he was convinced that we were on a pleasure cruise a few miles off Batavia.

The unfamiliar motion of the dinghy, as it rose and fell in the troughs between the waves, resulted in almost everyone getting seasick. As no one could eat anything, a day's rations were saved.

The sun was very hot, and my father covered my head with a large spotted handkerchief. He'd always had a fancy for bandana handkerchiefs with yellow spots, and seldom carried fewer than two on his person; so he had one for himself too. The sola topi, well soaked in sea water, was being used by Mr Muggeridge.

It was only when I had recovered to some extent from my seasickness that I remembered the valuable

stamp album, and sat up, exclaiming, 'The stamps! Did you bring the stamp album, Dad?'

He shook his head ruefully. 'It must be at the bottom of the sea by now,' he said. 'But don't worry, I kept a few rare stamps in my wallet.' And looking pleased with himself, he tapped the pocket of his bush shirt.

The dinghy drifted all day, with no one having the least idea where it might be taking us.

'Probably going round in circles,' said Mr Muggeridge pessimistically.

There was no compass and no sail, and paddling wouldn't have got us far even if we'd had paddles; we could only resign ourselves to the whims of the current and hope it would take us towards land or at least to within hailing distance of some passing ship.

The sun went down like an overripe tomato dissolving slowly in the sea. The darkness pressed down on us. It was a moonless night, and all we could see was the white foam on the crests of the waves. I lay with my head on my father's shoulder, and looked up at the stars which glittered in the remote heavens.

'Perhaps your friend Sono will look up at the sky tonight and see those same stars,' said my father. 'The world isn't so big after all.'

'All the same, there's a lot of sea around us,' said Mr Muggeridge from out of the darkness.

Remembering Sono, I put my hand in my pocket and was reassured to feel the smooth outline of the jade sea horse.

'I've still got Sono's sea horse,' I said, showing it to my father.

'Keep it carefully,' he said. 'It may bring us luck.'

'Are sea horses lucky?'

'Who knows? But he gave it to you with love, and love is like a prayer. So keep it carefully.'

I didn't sleep much that night. I don't think anyone slept. No one spoke much either, except, of course, Mr Muggeridge, who kept muttering something about cold beer and salami.

I didn't feel so sick the next day. By ten o'clock I was quite hungry; but breakfast consisted of two biscuits, a piece of chocolate, and a little drinking water. It was another hot day, and we were soon very thirsty, but everyone agreed that we should ration ourselves strictly.

Two or three still felt ill, but the others, including Mr Muggeridge, had recovered their appetites and normal spirits, and there was some discussion about the prospects of being picked up.

'Are there any distress rockets in the dinghy?' asked my father. 'If we see a ship or a plane, we can fire a rocket and hope to be spotted. Otherwise there's not much chance of our being seen from a distance.'

A thorough search was made in the dinghy, but there were no rockets.

'Someone must have used them last Guy Fawkes Day,' commented Mr Muggeridge.

'They don't celebrate Guy Fawkes Day in Holland,' said my father. 'Guy Fawkes was an Englishman.'

'Ah,' said Mr Muggeridge, not in the least put out. 'I've always said, most great men are Englishmen. And what did this chap Guy Fawkes do?'

'Tried to blow up Parliament,' said my father.

That afternoon we saw our first sharks. They were enormous creatures, and as they glided backward and forward under the boat it seemed they might hit and capsize us. They went away for some time, but returned in the evening.

At night, as I lay half asleep beside my father, I felt a few drops of water strike my face. At first I thought it was the sea spray; but when the sprinkling continued, I realized that it was raining lightly.

'Rain!' I shouted, sitting up. 'It's raining!'

Everyone woke up and did his best to collect water

in mugs, hats or other containers. Mr Muggeridge lay back with his mouth open, drinking the rain as it fell.

'This is more like it,' he said.

'You can have all the sun an' sand in the world. Give me a rainy day in England!'

But by early morning the clouds had passed, and the day turned out to be even hotter than the previous one. Soon we were all red and raw from sunburn. By midday even Mr Muggeridge was silent. No one had the energy to talk.

Then my father whispered, 'Can you hear a plane, lad?'

I listened carefully, and above the hiss of the waves I heard what sounded like the distant drone of a plane; it must have been very far away, because we could not see it. Perhaps it was flying into the sun, and the glare was too much for our sore eyes; or perhaps we'd just imagined the sound.

Then the Dutchman who'd lost his memory thought he saw land, and kept pointing towards the horizon and saying, 'That's Batavia, I told you we were close to shore!' No one else saw anything. So my father and I weren't the only ones imagining things.

Said my father, 'It only goes to show that a man

can see what he wants to see, even if there's nothing to be seen!'

The sharks were still with us. Mr Muggeridge began to resent them. He took off one of his shoes and hurled it at the nearest shark; but the big fish ignored the shoe and swam on after us.

'Now, if your leg had been in that shoe, Mr Muggeridge, the shark might have accepted it,' observed my father.

'Don't throw your shoes away,' said the captain. 'We might land on a deserted coastline and have to walk hundreds of miles!'

A light breeze sprang up that evening, and the dinghy moved more swiftly on the choppy water.

'At last we're moving forward,' said the captain.

'In circles,' said Mr Muggeridge.

But the breeze was refreshing; it cooled our burning limbs, and helped us to get some sleep. In the middle of the night I woke up feeling very hungry.

'Are you all right?' asked my father, who had been awake all the time.

'Just hungry,' I said.

'And what would you like to eat?'

'Oranges!'

He laughed. 'No oranges on board. But I kept a

piece of my chocolate for you. And there's a little water, if you're thirsty.' I kept the chocolate in my mouth for a long time, trying to make it last. Then I sipped a little water.

'Aren't you hungry?' I asked.

'Ravenous! I could eat a whole turkey. When we get to Bombay or Madras or Colombo, or wherever it is we get to, we'll go to the best restaurant in town and eat like—like—'

'Like shipwrecked sailors!' I said.

'Exactly.'

'Do you think we'll ever get to land, Dad?'

'I'm sure we will. You're not afraid, are you?'

'No. Not as long as you're with me.'

Next morning, to everyone's delight, we saw seagulls. This was a sure sign that land couldn't be far away; but a dinghy could take days to drift a distance of thirty or forty miles. The birds wheeled noisily above the dinghy. Their cries were the first familiar sounds we had heard for three days and three nights, apart from the wind and the sea and our own weary voices.

The sharks had disappeared, and that too was an encouraging sign. They didn't like the oil slicks that were appearing in the water.

But presently the gulls left us, and we feared we were drifting away from land.

'Circles,' repeated Mr Muggeridge. 'Circles.'

We had sufficient food and water for another week at sea; but no one even wanted to think about spending another week at sea.

The sun was a ball of fire. Our water ration wasn't sufficient to quench our thirst. By noon, we were without much hope or energy.

My father had his pipe in his mouth. He didn't have any tobacco, but he liked holding the pipe between his teeth. He said it prevented his mouth from getting too dry.

The sharks came back.

Mr Muggeridge removed his other shoe and threw it at them.

'Nothing like a lovely wet English summer,' he mumbled.

I fell asleep in the well of the dinghy, my father's large handkerchief spread over my face. The yellow spots on the cloth seemed to grow into enormous revolving suns.

When I woke up, I found a huge shadow hanging over us. At first I thought it was a cloud. But it was a shifting shadow. My father took the handkerchief from my face and said, 'You can wake up now, lad. We'll be home and dry soon.'

A fishing boat was beside us, and the shadow came from its wide, flapping sail. A number of bronzed, smiling, chattering fishermen—Burmese, as we discovered later—were gazing down at us from the deck of their boat.

A few days later my father and I were in Bombay. My father sold his rare stamps for over a thousand rupees, and we were able to live in a comfortable hotel. Mr Muggeridge was flown back to England. Later we got a postcard from him saying the English rain was awful!

'And what about us?' I asked. 'Aren't we going back to England?'

'Not yet,' said my father. 'You'll be going to a boarding school in Simla, until the war's over.'

'But why should I leave you?' I asked.

'Because I've joined the RAF,' he said.

'Don't worry, I'm being posted to Delhi. I'll be able to come up to see you sometimes.'

A week later I was on a small train which went chugging up the steep mountain track to Simla. Several Indian, Anglo-Indian and English children tumbled around in the compartment. I felt quite out of place among them, as though I had grown out of their pranks. But I wasn't unhappy. I knew my father would be coming to see me soon. He'd promised me some books, a pair of roller skates, and a cricket bat, just as soon as he got his first month's pay.

Meanwhile, I had the jade sea horse which Sono had given me.

And I have it with me today.

Sita and the River

The Island in the River

In the middle of the river, the river that began in the mountains of the Himalayas and ended in the Bay of Bengal, there was a small island. The river swept round the island, sometimes clawing at its banks but never going right over it. The river was still deep and swift at this point, because the foothills were only forty miles distant. More than twenty years had passed since the river had flooded the island, and at that time no one had lived there. But then years ago a small family had come to live on the island and now a small hut stood on it, a mud-walled hut with a sloping thatched roof. The hut had been built into a huge rock. Only three of its walls were mud, the fourth was rock.

A few goats grazed on the short grass and the prickly leaves of the thistle. Some hens followed them about. There was a melon patch and a vegetable patch and a small field of marigolds. The marigolds were sometimes made into garlands, and the garlands were sold during weddings or festivals in the nearby town.

In the middle of the island stood a peepul tree. It was the only tree on this tongue of land. But peepul trees will grow anywhere—through the walls of old temples, through gravestones, even from rooftops. It is usually the buildings, and not the trees, that give way!

Even during the great flood, which had occurred twenty years back, the peepul tree had stood firm.

It was an old tree, much older than the old man on the island, who was only seventy. The peepul was about three hundred. It provided shelter for the birds who sometimes visited it from the mainland.

Three hundred years ago, the land on which the peepul tree stood had been part of the mainland; but the river had changed its course and the bit of land with the tree on it had become an island. The tree had lived alone for many years. Now it gave shade and shelter to a small family who were grateful for its presence.

The people of India love peepul trees, especially during the hot summer months when the heart-shaped leaves catch the least breath of air and flutter eagerly, fanning those who sit beneath.

A sacred tree, the peepul, the abode of spirits, good and bad.

'Do not yawn when you are sitting beneath the tree,' Grandmother would warn Sita, her ten-year-old granddaughter. 'And if you must yawn, always snap your fingers in front of your mouth. If you forget to do that, a demon might jump down your throat!'

'And then what will happen?' asked Sita.

'He will probably ruin your digestion,' said Grandfather, who didn't take demons very seriously.

The peepul had beautiful leaves and Grandmother likened it to the body of the mighty god Krishna—broad at the shoulders, then tapering down to a very slim waist.

The tree attracted birds and insects from across the river. On some nights it was full of fireflies.

Whenever Grandmother saw the fireflies, she told her favourite story.

'When we first came here,' she said, 'we were greatly troubled by mosquitoes. One night your grandfather rolled himself up in his sheet so that they couldn't get at him. After a while he peeped out of his bedsheet to make sure they were gone. He saw a firefly and said, "You clever mosquito! You could not see in the dark, so you got a lantern!"'

Grandfather was mending a fishing net. He had

fished in the river for ten years, and he was a good fisherman. He knew where to find the slim silver chilwa and the big, beautiful mahseer and the singhara with its long whiskers; he knew where the river was deep and where it was shallow; he knew which baits to use—when to use worms and when to use gram. He had taught his son to fish, but his son had gone to work in a factory in a city nearly a hundred miles away. He had no grandson but he had a granddaughter, Sita, and she could do all the things a boy could do and sometimes she could do them better. She had lost her mother when she was two or three. Grandmother had taught her all that a girl should know—cooking, sewing, grinding spices, cleaning the house, feeding the birds—and Grandfather had taught her other things, like taking a small boat across the river, cleaning a fish, repairing a net, or catching a snake by the tail! And some things she had learnt by herself—like climbing the peepul tree, or leaping from rock to rock in shallow water, or swimming in an inlet where the water was calm.

Neither grandparent could read or write, and as a result Sita couldn't read or write.

There was a school in one of the villages across the river, but Sita had never seen it. She had never been further than Shahganj, the small market town near the river. She had never seen a city. She had never been in a train. The river cut her off from many things, but she could not miss what she had never known and, besides, she was much too busy.

While Grandfather mended his net, Sita was inside the hut, pressing her grandmother's forehead which was hot with fever. Grandmother had been ill for three days and could not eat. She had been ill before but she had never been so bad. Grandfather had brought her some sweet oranges but she couldn't take anything else.

She was younger than Grandfather but, because she was sick, she looked much older. She had never been very strong. She coughed a lot and sometimes she had difficulty in breathing.

When Sita noticed that Grandmother was sleeping, she left the bedside and tiptoed out of the room on her bare feet.

Outside, she found the sky dark with monsoon clouds. It had rained all night and, in a few hours, it would rain again. The monsoon rains had come early at the end of June. Now it was the end of July and already the river was swollen. Its rushing sounds seemed nearer and more menacing than usual.

Sita went to her grandfather and sat down beside him.

'When you are hungry, tell me,' she said, 'and I will make the bread.'

'Is your grandmother asleep?'

'Yes. But she will wake soon. The pain is deep.'

The old man stared out across the river, at the dark green of the forest, at the leaden sky, and said, 'If she is not better by morning, I will take her to the hospital in Shahganj. They will know how to make her well. You may be on your own for two or three days. You have been on your own before.'

Sita nodded gravely—she had been alone before; but not in the middle of the rains with the river so high. But she knew that someone must stay behind. She wanted Grandmother to get well and she knew that only Grandfather could take the small boat across the river when the current was so strong.

Sita was not afraid of being left alone, but she did not like the look of the river. That morning, when she had been fetching water, she had noticed that the lever had suddenly disappeared.

'Grandfather, if the river rises higher, what will I do?'

'You must keep to the high ground.'

'And if the water reaches the high ground?'

'Then go into the hut and take the hens with you.'

'And if the water comes into the hut?'

'Then climb into the peepul tree. It is a strong tree. It will not fall. And the water cannot rise higher than the tree.'

'And the goats, Grandfather?'

'I will be taking them with me. I may have to sell them, to pay for good food and medicine for your grandmother. As for the hens, you can put them on the roof if the water enters the hut. But do not worry too much,' and he patted Sita's head, 'the water will not rise so high. Has it ever done so? I will be back soon, remember that.'

'And won't Grandmother come back?'

'Yes—but they may keep her in the hospital for some time.'

The Sound of the River

That evening it began to rain again. Big pellets of rain, scarring the surface of the river. But it was warm rain and Sita could move about in it. She was not afraid of getting wet, she rather liked it. In the previous month, when the first monsoon shower had arrived, washing the dusty leaves of the tree and bringing up the good smell of the earth, she had exulted in it, had run about shouting for joy. She was used to it now, even a little tired of the rain, but she did not mind getting wet. It was steamy indoors and her thin dress would soon dry in the heat from the kitchen fire.

She walked about barefooted, barelegged. She was very sure on her feet. Her toes had grown accustomed to gripping all kinds of rocks, slippery or sharp, and though thin, she was surprisingly strong.

Black hair, streaming across her face. Black eyes. Slim brown arms. A scar on her thigh: when she was small, visiting her mother's village, a hyena had entered the house where she was sleeping, fastened on to her leg and tried to drag her away, but her screams had roused the villagers and the hyena had run off.

She moved about in the pouring rain, chasing the hens into a shelter behind the hut. A harmless brown snake, flooded out of its hole, was moving across the open ground. Sita took a stick, picked the snake up with it, and dropped it behind a cluster of rocks. She had no quarrel with snakes. They kept down the rats and the frogs. She wondered how the rats had first come to the island—probably in someone's boat or in a sack of grain.

She disliked the huge black scorpions which left their waterlogged dwellings and tried to take shelter in the hut. It was so easy to step on one and the sting could be very painful. She had been bitten by a scorpion the previous monsoon, and for a day and a night she had known fever and great pain. Sita had never killed living creatures but now, whenever she found a scorpion, she crushed it with a rock! When, finally, she went indoors, she was hungry. She ate some parched gram and warmed up some goat's milk.

Grandmother woke once and asked for water, and Grandfather held the brass tumbler to her lips.

It rained all night.

The roof was leaking and a small puddle formed on the floor. Grandfather kept the kerosene lamps alight. They did not need the light but somehow it made them feel safer.

The sound of the river had always been with them, although they seldom noticed it. But that night they noticed a change in its sound. There was something like a moan, like a wind in the tops of tall trees, and a swift hiss as the water swept round the rocks and carried away pebbles. And sometimes there was a rumble as loose earth fell into the water. Sita could not sleep.

She had a rag doll, made with Grandmother's help out of bits of old clothing. She kept it by her side every night. The doll was someone to talk to when the nights were long and sleep elusive. Her grandparents were often ready to talk but sometimes Sita wanted to have secrets, and though there were no special secrets in her life, she made up a few because it was fun to have them. And if you have secrets, you must have a friend to share them with. Since there were no other children on the island, Sita shared her secrets with the rag doll whose name was Mumta.

Grandfather and Grandmother were asleep, though the sound of Grandmother's laboured breathing was almost as persistent as the sound of the river.

'Mumta,' whispered Sita in the dark, starting one of her private conversations, 'do you think Grandmother will get well again?'

Mumta always answered Sita's questions, even though the answers were really Sita's answers.

'She is very old,' said Mumta.

'Do you think the river will reach the hut?' asked Sita.

'If it keeps raining like this and the river keeps rising, it will reach the hut.'

'I am afraid of the river, Mumta. Aren't you afraid?'

'Don't be afraid. The river has always been good to us.'

'What will we do if it comes into the hut?'

'We will climb on the roof.'

'And if it reaches the roof?'

'We will climb the peepul tree. The river has never gone higher than the peepul tree.'

As soon as the first light showed through the little skylight, Sita got up and went outside. It wasn't raining hard, it was drizzling; but it was the sort of drizzle that could continue for days, and it probably meant that heavy rain was falling in the hills where the river began.

Sita went down to the water's edge. She couldn't find her favourite rock, the one on which she often sat dangling her feet in the water, watching the little chilwa fish swim by. It was still there, no doubt, but the river had gone over it.

She stood on the sand and she could feel the water oozing and bubbling beneath her feet.

The river was no longer green and blue and flecked with white. It was a muddy colour.

Sita milked the goat thinking that perhaps it was the last time she would be milking it. But she did not care for the goat in the same way that she cared for Mumta.

The sun was just coming up when Grandfather pushed off in the boat. Grandmother lay in the prow. She was staring hard at Sita, trying to speak, but the words would not come. She raised her hand in blessing.

Sita bent and touched her grandmother's feet and then Grandfather pushed off. The little boat—with its two old people and three goats—rode swiftly on the river, edging its way towards the opposite bank. The current was very swift and the boat would be carried about half a mile downstream before Grandfather would be able to get it to dry land.

It bobbed about on the water, getting small and smaller, until it was just a speck on the broad river.

And suddenly Sita was alone.

There was a wind, whipping the raindrops against her face; and there was the water, rushing past the island; and there was the distant shore, blurred by rain; and there was the small hut; and there was the tree.

Sita got busy. The hens had to be fed. They weren't concerned about anything except food. Sita threw them a handful of coarse grain, potato peels and peanut shells.

Then she took the broom and swept out the hut, lit the charcoal burner, warmed some milk, and thought, 'Tomorrow there will be no milk . . .' She began peeling onions. Soon her eyes started smarting, and pausing for a few moments and glancing round the quiet room, she became aware again that she was alone. Grandfather's hookah pipe stood by itself in one corner. It was a beautiful old hookah, which had belonged to Sita's great-grandfather. The bowl was made out of a coconut encased in silver. The long, winding stem was at least four feet long. It was their most treasured possession. Grandmother's sturdy shisham-wood walking stick stood in another corner.

Sita looked around for Mumta, found the doll beneath the light wooden charpoy, and placed her within sight and hearing. Thunder rolled down from the hills. Boom—boom—boom . . .

'The gods of the mountains are angry,' said Sita. 'Do you think they are angry with me?'

'Why should they be angry with you?' asked Mumta.

'They don't need a reason for being angry. They are angry with everything and we are in the middle of everything. We are so small—do you think they know we are here?'

'Who knows what the gods think?'

'But I made you,' said Sita, 'and I know you are here.'

'And will you save me if the river rises?'

'Yes, of course. I won't go anywhere without you, Mumta.'

The Water Rises

Sita couldn't stay indoors for long. She went out, taking Mumta with her, and stared out across the river to the safe land on the other side. But was it really safe there? The river looked much wider now. It had crept over its banks and spread far across the flat plain. Far away, people were driving their cattle through waterlogged, flooded fields, carrying their belongings in bundles on their heads or shoulders, leaving their homes, making for high land. It wasn't safe anywhere.

Sita wondered what had happened to Grandfather and Grandmother. If they had reached the shore safely, Grandfather would have had to engage a bullock cart or a pony-drawn ekka to get Grandmother to the district hospital, five or six miles away. Shahganj had a market, a court, a jail, a cinema and a hospital.

She wondered if she would ever see Grandmother again. She had done her best to look after the old lady, remembering the times when Grandmother had looked after her, had gently touched her fevered brow, and had told her stories—stories about the gods—about the young Krishna, friend of birds and animals, so full of mischief, always causing confusion among the other gods. He made God Indra angry by shifting a mountain without permission. Indra was the god of the clouds, who made the thunder and lightning, and when he was angry he sent down a deluge such as this one.

The island looked much smaller now. Some of its mud banks had dissolved quickly, sinking into the river. But in the middle of the island there was rocky ground, and the rocks would never crumble; they could only be submerged.

Sita climbed into the tree to get a better view of the flood. She had climbed the tree many times, and it took her only a few seconds to reach the higher branches. She put her hand to her eyes as a shield from the rain and gazed upstream.

There was water everywhere. The world had become one vast river. Even the trees on the forested side of the river looked as though they had grown out of the water, like mangroves. The sky was banked with massive, moisture-laden clouds. Thunder rolled down from the hills, and the river seemed to take it up with a hollow booming sound.

Something was floating down the river, something big and bloated. It was closer now and Sita could make out its bulk—a drowned bullock being carried downstream.

So the water had already flooded the villages further upstream. Or perhaps, the bullock had strayed too close to the rising river.

Sita's worst fears were confirmed when, a little later, she saw planks of wood, small trees and bushes, and then a wooden bedstead, floating past the island.

As she climbed down from the tree, it began to rain more heavily. She ran indoors, shooing the hens before her. They flew into the hut and huddled under Grandmother's cot. Sita thought it would be best to keep them together now.

There were three hens and a cockbird. The river did not bother them. They were interested only in food, and Sita kept them content by throwing them a handful of onion skins.

She would have liked to close the door and shut out the swish of the rain and the boom of the river, but then she would have no way of knowing how fast the water rose.

She took Mumta in her arms, and began praying for the rain to stop and the river to fall. She prayed to God Indra, and just in case he was busy elsewhere, she prayed to other gods too. She prayed for the safety of her grandparents and for her own safety. She put herself last—but only after an effort!

Finally Sita decided to make herself a meal. So she chopped up some onions, fried them, then added turmeric and red chilli powder, salt and water, and stirred until she had everything sizzling; and then she added a cup of lentils and covered the pot.

Doing this took her about ten minutes. It would take about half an hour for the dish to cook.

When she looked outside, she saw pools of water among the rocks. She couldn't tell if it was rainwater or the overflow from the river.

She had an idea.

A big tin trunk stood in a corner of the room. In it Grandmother kept an old single-thread sewing machine. It had belonged once to an English lady, had found its way to a Shahganj junkyard, and had been rescued by Grandfather who had paid fifteen rupees for it. It was just over a hundred years old but it could still be used.

The trunk also contained an old sword. This had originally belonged to Sita's great-grandfather, who had used it to help defend his village against marauding Rohilla soldiers more than a century ago. Sita could tell that it had been used to fight with, because there were several small dents in the steel blade.

But there was no time for Sita to start admiring family heirlooms. She decided to stuff the trunk with everything useful or valuable. There was a chance that it wouldn't be carried away by the water.

Grandfather's hookah went into the trunk. Grandmother's walking stick went in, too. So did a number of small tins containing the spices used in cooking—nutmeg, caraway seed, cinnamon, coriander, pepper—also a big tin of flour and another of molasses. Even if she had to spend several hours in the tree, there would be something to eat when she came down again.

A clean white cotton dhoti of Grandfather's and Grandmother's only spare sari also went into the trunk. Never mind if they got stained with curry powder! Never mind if they got the smell of salted fish—some of that went in, too.

Sita was so busy packing the trunk that she paid no attention to the lick of cold water at her heels. She locked the trunk, dropped the key into a crack in the rock wall and turned to give her attention to the food. It was only then that she discovered that she was walking about on a watery floor.

She stood still, horrified by what she saw. The water was oozing over the threshold, pushing its way into the room.

In her fright, Sita forgot about her meal and everything else. Darting out of the hut, she ran splashing through ankle-deep water towards the safety of the peepul tree. If the tree hadn't been there, such a well-known landmark, she might have floundered into deep water, into the river.

She climbed swiftly into the strong arms of the tree, made herself comfortable on a familiar branch and thrust her wet hair away from her eyes.

The Tree

She was glad she had hurried. The hut was now surrounded by water. Only the higher parts of the island could still be seen—a few rocks, the big rock into which the hut was built, a hillock on which some brambles and thorn apples grew.

The hens hadn't bothered to leave the hut. Instead, they were perched on the wooden bedstead.

'Will the river rise still higher?' wondered Sita. She had never seen it like this before. With a deep, muffled roar it swirled around her, stretching away in all directions.

The most unusual things went by on the water—an aluminium kettle, a cane chair, a tin of tooth powder, an empty cigarette packet, a wooden slipper, a plastic doll . . .

A doll!

With a sinking feeling, Sita remembered Mumta.

Poor Mumta, she had been left behind in the hut. Sita, in her hurry, had forgotten her only companion.

She climbed down from the tree and ran splashing through the water towards the hut. Already the current was pulling at her legs. When she reached the hut, she found it full of water. The hens had gone and so had Mumta.

Sita struggled back to the tree. She was only just in time, for the waters were higher now, the island fast disappearing.

She crouched miserably in the fork of the tree, watching her world disappear.

She had always loved the river. Why was it threatening her now? She remembered the doll and thought, 'If I can be so careless with someone I have made, how can I expect the gods to notice me?'

Something went floating past the tree. Sita caught a glimpse of a stiff, upraised arm and long hair streaming behind on the water. The body of a drowned woman. It was soon gone but it made Sita feel very small and lonely, at the mercy of great and cruel forces. She began to shiver and then to cry.

She stopped crying when she saw an empty kerosene tin, with one of the hens perched on top. The tin came bobbing along on the water and sailed slowly past the tree. The hen looked a bit ruffled but seemed secure on its perch.

A little later, Sita saw the remaining hens fly up to the rock ledge to huddle there in a small recess.

The water was still rising. All that remained of the island was the big rock behind the hut and the top of the hut and the peepul tree.

She climbed a little higher into the crook of a branch. A jungle crow settled in the branches above her. Sita saw the nest, the crow's nest, an untidy platform of twigs wedged in the fork of a branch.

In the nest were four speckled eggs. The crow sat on them and cawed disconsolately. But though the bird sounded miserable, its presence brought some cheer to Sita. At least she was not alone. Better to have a crow for company than no one at all.

Other things came floating out of the hut—a large pumpkin; a red turban belonging to Grandfather, unwinding in the water like a long snake; and then—Mumta!

The doll, being filled with straw and wood shavings, moved quite swiftly on the water, too swiftly for Sita to do anything about rescuing it. Sita wanted to call out, to urge her friend to make for the tree, but she knew that Mumta could not swim—the doll could only float, travel with the river, and perhaps be washed ashore many miles downstream.

The trees shook in the wind and rain. The crow cawed and flew up, circled the tree a few times, then returned to the nest. Sita clung to the branch.

The tree trembled throughout its tall frame. To Sita it felt like an earthquake tremor. She felt the shudder of the tree in her own bones.

The river swirled all around her now. It was almost up to the roof of the hut. Soon the mud walls would crumble and vanish. Except for the big rock and some trees very far away, there was only water to be seen. Water and the grey, weeping sky.

In the distance, a boat with several people in it moved sluggishly away from the ruins of a flooded village. Someone looked out across the flooded river and said, 'See, there is a tree right in the middle of the river! How could it have got there? Isn't someone moving in the tree?'

But the others thought he was imagining things. It was only a tree carried down by the flood, they said. In worrying about their own distress, they had forgotten about the island in the middle of the river.

The river was very angry now, rampaging down from the hills and thundering across the plain, bringing with it dead animals, uprooted trees, household goods and huge fish choked to death by the swirling mud.

The peepul tree groaned. Its long, winding roots still clung tenaciously to the earth from which it had sprung many, many years ago. But the earth was softening, the stones were being washed away. The roots of the tree were rapidly losing their hold.

The crow must have known that something was wrong, because it kept flying up and circling the tree, reluctant to settle in it, yet unwilling to fly away. As long as the nest was there, the crow would remain too.

Sita's wet cotton dress clung to her thin body. The rain streamed down from her long, black hair. It poured from every leaf of the tree. The crow, too, was drenched and groggy.

The tree groaned and moved again.

There was a flurry of leaves, then a surge of mud from below. To Sita it seemed as though the river was rising to meet the sky. The tree tilted, swinging Sita from side to side. Her feet were in the water but she clung tenaciously to her branch.

And then, she found the tree moving, moving with the river, rocking her about, dragging its roots along the ground as it set out on the first and last journey of its life.

And as the tree moved out on the river and the little island was lost in the swirling waters, Sita forgot her fear and her loneliness. The tree was taking her with it. She was not alone. It was as though one of the gods had remembered her after all.

Taken with the Flood

The branches swung Sita about, but she did not lose her grip. The tree was her friend. It had known her all these years and now it held her in its old and dying arms as though it was determined to keep her from the river.

The crow kept flying around the moving tree. The bird was in a great rage. Its nest was still up there— but not for long! The tree lurched and twisted and the nest fell into the water. Sita saw the eggs sink.

The crow swooped low over the water, but there was nothing it could do. In a few moments the nest had disappeared.

The bird followed the tree for sometime. Then, flapping its wings, it rose high into the air and flew across the river until it was out of sight.

Sita was alone once more. But there was no time for feeling lonely. Everything was in motion—up and down and sideways and forwards.

She saw a turtle swimming past—a great big river turtle, the kind that feeds on decaying flesh. Sita turned her face away. In the distance she saw a flooded village and people in flat-bottomed boats; but they were very far.

Because of its great size, the tree did not move very swiftly on the river. Sometimes, when it reached shallow water, it stopped, its roots catching in the rocks. But not for long; the river's momentum soon swept it on.

At one place, where there was a bend in the river, the tree struck a sandbank and was still. It would not move again.

Sita felt very tired. Her arms were aching and she had to cling tightly to her branch to avoid slipping into the water. The rain blurred her vision. She wondered if she should brave the current and try swimming to safety. But she did not want to leave the tree. It was all that was left to her now, and she felt safe in its branches.

Then, above the sound of the river, she heard someone calling. The voice was faint and seemed very far, but looking upriver through the curtain of rain, Sita was able to make out a small boat coming towards her.

There was a boy in the boat. He seemed quite at home in the turbulent river, and he was smiling at Sita as he guided his boat towards the tree. He held on to one of the branches to steady himself and gave his free hand to Sita.

She grasped the outstretched hand and slipped into the boat beside the boy.

He placed his bare foot against the trunk of the tree and pushed away.

The little boat moved swiftly down the river. Sita looked back and saw the big tree lying on its side on the sandbank, while the river swirled round it and pulled at its branches, carrying away its beautiful, slender leaves.

And then the tree grew smaller and was left far behind. A new journey had begun.

The Boy in the Boat

She lay stretched out in the boat, too tired to talk, too tired to move. The boy looked at her but did not say anything. He just kept smiling. He leant on his two small oars, stroking smoothly, rhythmically, trying to keep from going into the middle of the river. He wasn't strong enough to get the boat right out of the swift current, but he kept trying.

A small boat on a big river—a river that had broken its bounds and reached across the plains in every direction—the boat moved swiftly on the wild brown water, and the girl's home and the boy's home were both left far behind.

The boy wore only a loincloth. He was a slim, wiry boy, with a hard, flat belly. He had high cheekbones and strong white teeth. He was a little darker than Sita.

He did not speak until they reached a broader, smoother stretch of river, and then, resting on his oars and allowing the boat to drift a little, he said, 'You live on the island. I have seen you sometimes from my boat. But where are the others?'

'My grandmother was sick,' said Sita. 'Grandfather took her to the hospital in Shahganj.'

'When did they leave?'

'Early this morning.'

Early that morning—and already Sita felt as though it had been many mornings ago!

'Where are you from?' she asked.

'I am from a village near the foothills. About six miles from your home. I was in my boat, trying to get across the river with the news that our village was badly flooded. The current was too strong. I was swept down and past your island. We cannot fight the river when it is like this, we must go where it takes us.'

'You must be tired,' said Sita. 'Give me the oars.'

'No. There is not much to do now. The river has gone wherever it wanted to go—it will not drive us before it any more.'

He brought in one oar, and with his free hand felt under the seat where there was a small basket. He produced two mangoes and gave one to Sita.

'I was supposed to sell these in Shahganj,' he said.

'My father is very strict. Even if I return home safely, he will ask me what I got for the mangoes!'

'And what will you tell him?'

'I will say they are at the bottom of the river!'

They bit deep into the ripe, fleshy mangoes, using their teeth to tear the skin away. The sweet juice trickled down their skins. The good smell—like the smell of the leaves of the cosmos flower when crushed between the palms—helped to revive Sita. The flavour of the fruit was heavenly—truly the nectar of the gods!

Sita hadn't tasted a mango for over a year. For a few moments she forgot about everything else. All that mattered was the sweet, dizzy flavour of the mango.

The boat drifted, but slowly now, for as they went further downstream, the river gradually lost its power and fury. It was late afternoon when the rain stopped, but the clouds did not break up.

'My father has many buffaloes,' said the boy, 'but several have been lost in the flood.'

'Do you go to school?' asked Sita.

'Yes, I am supposed to go to school. I don't always go. At least not when the weather is fine! There is a school near our village. I don't think you go to school?'

'No. There is too much work at home.'

'Can you read and write?'

'Only a little . . .'

'Then you should go to a school.'

'It is too far away.'

'True. But you should know how to read and write. Otherwise, you will be stuck on your island for the rest of your life—that is, if your island is still there!'

'But I like the island,' protested Sita.

'Because you are with people you love,' said the boy. 'But your grandparents, they are old, they must die some day—and then you will be alone, and will you like the island then?'

Sita did not answer. She was trying to think of what life would be like without her grandparents. It would be an empty island, that was true. She would be imprisoned by the river.

'I can help you,' said the boy. 'When we get back—
if we get back—I will come to see you sometimes and
I will teach you to read and write. All right?'

'Yes,' said Sita, nodding thoughtfully. When we
get back . . .

The boy smiled.

'My name is Vijay,' he said.

Towards evening the river changed colour. The sun,
low in the sky, broke through a rift in the clouds, and
the river changed slowly from grey to gold, from gold
to a deep orange, and then, as the sun went down,
all these colours were drowned in the river, and the
river took the colour of night.

The moon was almost at the full, and they could
see a belt of forest along the line of the river.

'I will try to reach the trees,' said Vijay.

He pulled for the trees, and after ten minutes of
strenuous rowing reached a bend in the river and was
able to escape the pull of the main current.

Soon they were in a forest, rowing between tall
trees of sal and shisham.

The boat moved slowly as Vijay took it in and out
of the trees, while the moonlight made a crooked
silver path over the water.

'We will tie the boat to a tree,' he said. 'Then we can rest. Tomorrow, we will have to find a way out of the forest.'

He produced a length of rope from the bottom of the boat, tied one end to the boat's stern, and threw the other end over a stout branch which hung only a few feet above the water. The boat came to rest against the trunk of the tree.

It was a tall, sturdy tree, the Indian mahogany. It was a safe place, for there was no rush of water in the forest and the trees grew close together, making the earth firm and unyielding.

But those who lived in the forest were on the move. The animals had been flooded out of their homes, caves and lairs, and were looking for shelter and high ground.

Sita and Vijay had just finished tying the boat to the tree, when they saw a huge python gliding over the water towards them.

'Do you think it will try to get into the boat?' asked Sita.

'I don't think so,' said Vijay, although he took the precaution of holding an oar ready to fend off the snake.

But the python went past them, its head above water, its great length trailing behind, until it was lost in the shadows.

Vijay had more mangoes in the basket, and he and Sita sucked hungrily on them while they sat in the boat.

A big sambhar stag came threshing through the water. He did not have to swim. He was so tall that his head and shoulders remained well above the water. His antlers were big and beautiful.

'There will be other animals,' said Sita. 'Should we climb on to the tree?'

'We are quite safe in the boat,' said Vijay. 'The animals will not be dangerous tonight. They will not even hunt each other. They are only interested in reaching dry land. For once, the deer are safe from the tiger and the leopard. You lie down and sleep. I will keep watch.'

Sita stretched herself out in the boat and closed her eyes. She was very tired and the sound of the water lapping against the side of the boat soon lulled her to sleep.

She woke once, when a strange bird called overhead. She raised herself on one elbow but Vijay

was awake, sitting beside her, his legs drawn up and his chin resting on his knees. He was gazing out across the water. He looked blue in the moonlight, the colour of the young God Krishna, and for a few moments Sita was confused and wondered if the boy was actually Krishna. But when she thought about it, she decided that it wasn't possible; he was just a village boy and she had seen hundreds like him—well, not exactly like him, he was a little different . . .

And when she slept again, she dreamt that the boy and Krishna were one, and that she was sitting beside him on a great white bird, which flew over the mountains, over the snow peaks of the Himalayas, into the cloud-land of the gods. And there was a great rumbling sound, as though the gods were angry about the whole thing, and she woke up to this terrible sound and looked about her, and there in the moonlit glade, up to his belly in water, stood a young elephant, his trunk raised as he trumpeted his predicament to the forest—for he was a young elephant, and he was lost, and was looking for his mother.

He trumpeted again, then lowered his head and listened. And presently, from far away, came the shrill trumpeting of another elephant. It must have been the young one's mother, because he gave several excited trumpet calls, and then went stamping and churning through the water towards a gap in the trees. The boat rocked in the waves made by his passing.

'It is all right,' said Vijay. 'You can go to sleep again.'

'I don't think I will sleep now,' said Sita.

'Then I will play my flute for you and the time will pass quickly.'

He produced a flute from under the seat and putting it to his lips began to play. And the sweetest music that Sita had ever heard came pouring from the little flute, and it seemed to fill the forest with its beautiful sound. And the music carried her away again, into the land of dreams, and they were riding on the bird once more, Sita and the blue god. And they were passing through cloud and mist, until suddenly the sun shot through the clouds. And at that moment Sita opened her eyes and saw the sky through the branches of the mahogany tree, the shiny green leaves making a bold pattern against the blinding blue of an open sky.

The forest was drenched with sunshine. Clouds were gathering again, but for an hour or so there would be a hot sun on a steamy river.

Vijay was fast asleep in the bottom of the boat. His flute lay in the palm of his half-open hand. The sun came slanting across his bare brown legs. A leaf had fallen on his face, but it had not woken him. It lay on his cheek as though it had grown there.

Sita did not move about as she did not want to wake the boy. Instead she looked around her, and thought the water level had fallen in the night, but she couldn't be sure.

Vijay woke at last. He yawned, stretched his limbs and sat up beside Sita.

'I am hungry,' he said.

'So am I,' said Sita.

'The last mangoes,' he said, emptying the basket of its last two mangoes.

After they had finished the fruit, they sucked the big seeds until they were quite dry. The discarded seeds floated well on the water. Sita had always preferred them to paper boats.

'We had better move on,' said Vijay.

He rowed the boat through the trees, and then for about an hour they were passing through the flooded forest, under the dripping branches of rain-washed trees. Sometimes, they had to use the oars to push away vines and creepers. Sometimes, submerged bushes hampered them. But they were out of the forest before ten o'clock.

The water was no longer very deep and they were soon gliding over flooded fields. In the distance they saw a village standing on high ground. In the old days, people had built their villages on hilltops as a better defence against bandits and the soldiers of invading armies. This was an old village, and though its inhabitants had long ago exchanged their swords for pruning forks, the hill on which it stood gave it protection from the flood waters.

A Bullock Cart Ride

The people of the village were at first reluctant to help Sita and Vijay.

'They are strangers,' said an old woman. 'They are not of our people.'

'They are of low caste,' said another. 'They cannot remain with us.'

'Nonsense!' said a tall, turbaned farmer, twirling his long, white moustache. 'They are children, not robbers. They will come into my house.'

The people of the village—long-limbed, sturdy men and women of the Jat race—were generous by nature, and once the elderly farmer had given them the lead, they were friendly and helpful.

Sita was anxious to get to her grandparents, and the farmer, who had business to transact at a village fair some twenty miles distant, offered to take Sita and Vijay with him.

The fair was being held at a place called Karauli, and at Karauli there was a railway station from which a train went to Shahganj.

It was a journey that Sita would always remember. The bullock cart was so slow on the waterlogged roads that there was plenty of time in which to see things, to notice one another, to talk, to think, to dream.

Vijay couldn't sit still in the cart. He was used to the swift, gliding movements of his boat (which he had had to leave behind in the village), and every now and then he would jump off the cart and walk beside it, often ankle-deep in water.

There were four of them in the cart. Sita and Vijay, Hukam Singh, the Jat farmer, and his son, Phambiri, a mountain of a man who was going to take part in the wrestling matches at the fair.

Hukam Singh, who drove the bullocks, liked to talk. He had been a soldier in the British Indian army during the First World War, and had been with his regiment to Italy and Mesopotamia.

'There is nothing to compare with soldiering,' he said, 'except, of course, farming. If you can't be a farmer, be a soldier. Are you listening, boy? Which will you be—farmer or soldier?'

'Neither,' said Vijay. 'I shall be an engineer!'

Hukam Singh's long moustache seemed almost to bristle with indignation.

'An engineer! What next! What does your father do, boy?'

'He keeps buffaloes.'

'Ah! And his son would be an engineer? . . . Well, well, the world isn't what it used to be! No one knows his rightful place any more. Men send their children to schools and what is the result? Engineers! And who will look after the buffaloes while you are engineering?'

'I will sell the buffaloes,' said Vijay, adding rather cheekily, 'perhaps you will buy one of them, Subedar Sahib!'

He took the cheek out of his remark by adding 'Subedar Sahib', the rank of a non-commissioned officer in the old army. Hukam Singh, who had never reached this rank, was naturally flattered.

'Fortunately, Phambiri hasn't been to school. He'll be a farmer and a fine one, too.'

Phambiri simply grunted, which could have meant anything. He hadn't studied further than class 6, which was just as well, as he was a man of muscle, not brain.

Phambiri loved putting his strength to some practical and useful purpose. Whenever the cart wheels got stuck in the mud, he would get off, remove his shirt and put his shoulder to the side of the cart, while his muscles bulged and the sweat glistened on his broad back.

'Phambiri is the strongest man in our district,' said Hukam Singh proudly. 'And clever, too! It takes quick thinking to win a wrestling match.'

'I have never seen one,' said Sita.

'Then stay with us tomorrow morning, and you will see Phambiri wrestle. He has been challenged by the Karauli champion. It will be a great fight!'

'We must see Phambiri win,' said Vijay.

'Will there be time?' asked Sita.

'Why not? The train for Shahganj won't come in till evening. The fair goes on all day and the wrestling bouts will take place in the morning.'

'Yes, you must see me win!' exclaimed Phambiri, thumping himself on the chest as he climbed back on to the cart after freeing the wheels. 'No one can defeat me!'

'How can you be so certain?' asked Vijay.

'He has to be certain,' said Hukam Singh. 'I have taught him to be certain! You can't win anything if you are uncertain . . . Isn't that right, Phambiri? You know you are going to win!'

'I know,' said Phambiri with a grunt of confidence.

'Well, someone has to lose,' said Vijay.

'Very true,' said Hukam Singh smugly. 'After all, what would we do without losers? But for Phambiri, it is win, win, all the time!'

'And if he loses?' persisted Vijay.

'Then he will just forget that it happened and will go on to win his next fight!'

Vijay found Hukam Singh's logic almost unanswerable, but Sita, who had been puzzled by the argument, now saw everything very clearly and said, 'Perhaps he hasn't won any fights as yet. Did he lose the last one?'

'Hush!' said Hukam Singh looking alarmed. 'You must not let him remember. You do not remember losing a fight, do you, my son?'

'I have never lost a fight,' said Phambiri with great simplicity and confidence.

'How strange,' said Sita. 'If you lose, how can you win?'

'Only a soldier can explain that,' said Hukam Singh. 'For a man who fights, there is no such thing as defeat. You fought against the river, did you not?'

'I went with the river,' said Sita. 'I went where it took me.'

'Yes, and you would have gone to the bottom if the boy had not come along to help you. He fought the river, didn't he?'

'Yes, he fought the river,' said Sita.

'You helped me to fight it,' said Vijay.

'So you both fought,' said the old man with a nod of satisfaction. 'You did not go with the river. You did not leave everything to the gods.'

'The gods were with us,' said Sita.

And so they talked, while the bullock cart trundled along the muddy village roads. Both bullocks were white, and were decked out for the fair with coloured bead necklaces and bells hanging from their necks. They were patient, docile beasts. But the cartwheels which were badly in need of oiling, protested loudly, creaking and groaning as though all the demons in the world had been trapped within them.

Sita noticed a number of birds in the paddy fields. There were black-and-white curlews and cranes with pink coat-tails. A good monsoon means plenty of birds. But Hukam Singh was not happy about the cranes.

'They do great damage in the wheat fields,' he said. Lighting up a small, hand-held hookah pipe, he puffed at it and became philosophical again: 'Life is one long struggle for the farmer. When he has overcome the drought, survived the flood, hunted off the pig, killed the crane and reaped the crop, then comes that blood-sucking ghoul, the moneylender. There is no escaping him! Is your father in debt to a moneylender, boy?'

'No,' said Vijay.

'That is because he doesn't have daughters who must be married! I have two. As they resemble Phambiri, they will need generous dowries.'

In spite of his grumbling, Hukam Singh seemed fairly content with his lot. He'd had a good maize crop, and the front of his cart was piled high with corn. He would sell the crop at the fair, along with some cucumbers, eggplants and melons.

The bad road had slowed them down so much that when darkness came, they were still far from Karauli. In India there is hardly any twilight. Within a short time of the sun's going down, the stars come out.

'Six miles to go,' said Hukam Singh. 'In the dark

our wheels may get stuck again. Let us spend the night here. If it rains, we can pull an old tarpaulin over the cart.'

Vijay made a fire in the charcoal burner which Hukam Singh had brought along, and they had a simple meal, roasting the corn over the fire and flavouring it with salt and spices and a squeeze of lemon. There was some milk, but not enough for everyone because Phambiri drank three tumblers by himself.

'If I win tomorrow,' he said, 'I will give all of you a feast!'

They settled down to sleep in the bullock cart, and Phambiri and his father were soon snoring. Vijay lay awake, his arms crossed behind his head, staring up at the stars. Sita was very tired but she couldn't sleep. She was worrying about her grandparents and wondering when she would see them again.

The night was full of sounds. The loud snoring that came from Phambiri and his father seemed to be taken up by invisible sleepers all around them, and Sita, becoming alarmed, turned to Vijay and asked, 'What is that strange noise?'

He smiled in the darkness, and she could see his white teeth and the glint of laughter in his eyes.

'Only the spirits of lost demons,' he said, and then laughed. 'Can't you recognize the music of the frogs?'

And that was what they heard—a sound more hideous than the wail of demons, a rising crescendo of noise—wurrk, wurrk, wurrk—coming from the flooded ditches on either side of the road. All the frogs in the jungle seemed to have gathered at that one spot, and each one appeared to have something to say for himself. The speeches continued for about an hour. Then the meeting broke up and silence returned to the forest.

A jackal slunk across the road. A puff of wind brushed through the trees. The bullocks, freed from the cart, were asleep beside it. The men's snores were softer now. Vijay slept, a half-smile on his face. Only Sita lay awake, worried and waiting for the dawn.

At the Fair

Already, at nine o'clock, the fairground was crowded. Cattle were being sold or auctioned. Stalls had opened, selling everything from pins to ploughs. Foodstuffs were on sale—hot food, spicy food, sweets and ices. A merry-go-round, badly oiled, was squeaking and groaning, while a loudspeaker blared popular film music across the grounds.

While Phambiri was preparing for his wrestling match, Hukam Singh was busy haggling over the price of pumpkins. Sita and Vijay wandered on their own among the stalls, gazing at toys and kites and bangles and clothing, at brightly coloured syrupy sweets. Some of the rural people had transistor radios dangling by straps from their shoulders, the radio music competing with the loudspeaker. Occasionally a buffalo bellowed, drowning all other sounds.

Various people were engaged in roadside professions. There was the fortune teller. He had slips of paper, each of them covered with writing, which he kept in little trays along with some grain. He had a tame sparrow. When you gave the fortune teller your money, he allowed the little bird to hop in and out among the trays until it stopped at one and started pecking at the grain. From this tray the fortune teller took the slip of paper and presented it to his client. The writing told you what to expect over the next few months or years.

A harassed, middle-aged man, who was surrounded by six noisy sons and daughters, was looking a little concerned because his slip of paper said: 'Do not lose hope. You will have a child soon.'

Some distance away sat a barber, and near him a professional ear cleaner. Several children clustered around a peepshow, which was built into an old gramophone cabinet. While one man wound up the gramophone and placed a well-worn record on the turntable, his partner pushed coloured pictures through a slide viewer.

A young man walked energetically up and down the fairground, beating a drum and announcing the day's attractions. The wrestling bouts were about to start. The main attraction was going to be the fight between Phambiri, described as a man 'whose thighs had the thickness of an elephant's trunk', and the local champion, Sher Dil (tiger's heart)—a wild-looking man, with hairy chest and beetling brow. He was heavier than Phambiri but not so tall.

Sita and Vijay joined Hukam Singh at one corner of the akhara, the wrestling pit. Hukam Singh was massaging his son's famous thighs.

A gong sounded and Sher Dil entered the ring, slapping himself on the chest and grunting like a wild boar. Phambiri advanced slowly to meet him.

They came to grips immediately, and stood swaying

from side to side, two giants pitting their strength against each other. The sweat glistened on their well-oiled bodies.

Sher Dil got his arms round Phambiri's waist and tried to lift him off his feet, but Phambiri had twined one powerful leg around his opponent's thigh, and they both came down together with a loud squelch, churning up the soft mud of the wrestling pit. But neither wrestler had been pinned down.

Soon they were so covered with mud that it was difficult to distinguish one from the other. There was a flurry of arms and legs. The crowd was cheering and Sita and Vijay were cheering too, but the wrestlers were too absorbed in their struggle to be aware of their supporters. Each sought to turn the other on to his back. That was all that mattered. There was no count.

For a few moments Sher Dil had Phambiri almost helpless, but Phambiri wriggled out of a crushing grip, and using his legs once again, sent Sher Dil rocketing across the akhara. But Sher Dil landed on his belly, and even with Phambiri on top of him, it wasn't victory.

Nothing happened for several minutes, and the crowd became restless and shouted for more action. Phambiri thought of twisting his opponent's ear but he realized that he might get disqualified for doing that, so he restrained himself. He relaxed his grip slightly, and this gave Sher Dil a chance to heave himself up and send Phambiri spinning across the akhara. Phambiri was still in a sitting position when the other took a flying leap at him. But Phambiri dived forward, taking his opponent between the legs, and then rising, flung him backwards with a resounding thud. Sher Dil was helpless, and Phambiri sat on his opponent's chest to remove all doubts as to who was the winner. Only when the applause of the spectators told him that he had won did he rise and leave the ring.

Accompanied by his proud father, Phambiri accepted the prize money, thirty rupees, and then went in search of a tap. After he had washed the oil and mud from his body, he put on fresh clothes. Then, putting his arms around Vijay and Sita, he said, 'You have brought me luck, both of you. Now let us celebrate!' And he led the way to the sweet shops.

They ate syrupy rasgullas (made from milk and sugar) and almond-filled fudge, and little pies filled with minced meat, and washed everything down with a fizzy orange drink.

'Now I will buy each of you a small present,' said Phambiri.

He bought a bright blue sports shirt for Vijay. He bought a new hookah bowl for his father. And he took Sita to a stall where dolls were sold, and asked her to choose one.

There were all kinds of dolls—cheap plastic dolls, and beautiful dolls made by hand, dressed in the traditional costumes of different regions of the country. Sita was immediately reminded of Mumta, her own rag doll, who had been made at home with Grandmother's help. And she remembered Grandmother, and Grandmother's sewing machine, and the home that had been swept away, and the tears started to her eyes.

The dolls seemed to smile at Sita. The shopkeeper held them up one by one, and they appeared to dance, to twirl their wide skirts, to stamp their jingling feet on the counter. Each doll made her own special appeal to Sita. Each one wanted her love.

'Which one will you have?' asked Phambiri. 'Choose the prettiest, never mind the price!'

But Sita could say nothing. She could only shake her head. No doll, no matter how beautiful, could replace Mumta. She would never keep a doll again. That part of her life was over.

So instead of a doll Phambiri bought her bangles—

coloured glass bangles which slipped easily on Sita's thin wrists. And then he took them into a temporary cinema, a large shed made of corrugated tin sheets.

Vijay had been to a cinema before—the towns were full of cinemas—but for Sita it was another new experience. Many things that were common enough for other boys and girls were strange and new for a girl who had spent nearly all her life on a small island in the middle of a big river.

As they found seats, a curtain rolled up and a white sheet came into view. The babble of talk dwindled into silence. Sita became aware of a whirring noise somewhere not far behind her. But, before she could turn her head to see what it was, the sheet became a rectangle of light and colour. It came to life. People moved and spoke. A story unfolded.

But, long afterwards, all that Sita could remember of her first film was a jumble of images and incidents. A train in danger, the audience murmuring with anxiety, a bridge over a river (but smaller than hers), the bridge being blown to pieces, the engine plunging into the river, people struggling in the water, a woman rescued by a man who immediately embraced her, the lights coming on again, and the audience rising slowly and drifting out of the theatre, looking quite unconcerned and even satisfied. All those people struggling in the water were now quite safe, back in the little black box in the projection room.

Catching the Train

And now a real engine, a steam engine belching smoke and fire, was on its way towards Sita.

She stood with Vijay on the station platform along with over a hundred other people waiting for the Shahganj train.

The platform was littered with the familiar bedrolls (or holdalls) without which few people in India ever travel. On these rolls sat women, children, great-aunts and great-uncles, grandfathers, grandmothers and grandchildren, while the more active adults hovered at the edge of the platform, ready to leap on to the train as soon as it arrived and reserve a space for the family. In India, people do not travel alone if they can help it. The whole family must be taken along—especially if the reason for the journey is a marriage, a pilgrimage, or simply a visit to friends or relations.

Moving among the piles of bedding and luggage were coolies; vendors of magazines, sweetmeats, tea and betel-leaf preparations; also stray dogs, stray people and sometimes a stray stationmaster! The cries of the vendors mingled with the general clamour of the station and the shunting of a steam engine in the yard—'Tea, hot tea!', 'Fresh limes!' Sweets, papads, hot stuff, cold drinks, mangoes, toothpowder, photos of film stars, bananas, balloons, wooden toys! The platform had become a bazaar. What a blessing for those vendors that trains ran late and that people had to wait, and waiting, drank milky tea, bought toys for children, cracked peanut shells, munched bananas and chose little presents for the friends or relations on whom they were going to descend very shortly.

But there came the train!

The signal was down. The crowd surged forward, swamping an assistant stationmaster. Vijay took Sita by the hand and led her forward. If they were too slow, they would not get a place on the crowded train. In front of them was a tall, burly, bearded Sikh from the Punjab. Vijay decided it would be a wise move to stand behind him and move forward at the same time.

The station bell clanged and a big, puffing, black steam engine appeared in the distance. A stray dog, with a lifetime's experience of trains, darted away across the railway lines. As the train came alongside the platform, doors opened, window shutters fell, eager faces appeared in the openings, and even before the train had come to a stop, people were trying to get in or out.

For a few moments there was chaos. The crowd surged backwards and forwards. No one could get out. No one could get in! Fifty people were leaving the train, a hundred were catching it! No one wanted to give way. But every problem has a solution somewhere, provided one looks for it. And this particular problem was solved by a man climbing out of a window. Others followed his example. The pressure at the doors eased and people started squeezing into the compartments.

Vijay stayed close to the Sikh who forged a way through the throng. The Sikh reached an open doorway and was through. Vijay and Sita were through! They found somewhere to sit and were then able to look down at the platform, into the whirlpool and enjoy themselves a little. The vendors had abandoned the people on the platform and had started selling their wares at the windows. Hukam Singh, after buying their tickets, had given Vijay and Sita a rupee to spend on the way. Vijay bought a freshly split coconut, and Sita bought a comb for her hair. She had never bothered with her hair before.

They saw a worried man rushing along the platform searching for his family; but they were already in the compartment, having beaten him to it, and eagerly helped him in at the door. A whistle shrilled and they were off! A couple of vendors made last-minute transactions, then jumped from the slow-moving train. One man did this expertly with a tray of teacups balanced on one hand.

The train gathered speed.

'What will happen to all those people still on the platform?' asked Sita anxiously. 'Will they all be left behind?'

She put her head out of the window and looked back at the receding platform. It was strangely empty. Only the vendors and the coolies and the stray dogs and the dishevelled railway staff were in evidence. A miracle had happened. No one—absolutely no one—had been left behind!

Then the train was rushing through the night, the engine throwing out bright sparks that danced away like fireflies. Sometimes the train had to slow down, as flood water had weakened the embankments. Sometimes it stopped at brightly-lit stations.

When the train started again and moved on into the dark countryside, Sita would stare through the glass of the window, at the bright lights of a town or the quiet glow of village lamps. She thought of Phambiri and Hukam Singh, and wondered if she would ever see them again. Already they were like people in a fairy tale, met briefly on the road and never seen again.

There was no room in the compartment in which to lie down; but Sita soon fell asleep, her head resting against Vijay's shoulder.

A Meeting and a Parting

Sita did not know where to look for her grandfather. For an hour she and Vijay wandered through the Shahganj bazaar, growing hungrier all the time. They had no money left and they were hot and thirsty.

Outside the bazaar, near a small temple, they saw a tree in which several small boys were helping themselves to the sour, purple fruit.

It did not take Vijay long to join the boys in the tree. They did not object to his joining them. It wasn't their tree, anyway.

Sita stood beneath the tree while Vijay threw the jamuns down to her. They soon had a small pile of the fruit. They were on the road again, their faces stained with purple juice.

They were asking the way to the Shahganj hospital, when Sita caught a glimpse of her grandfather on the road.

At first the old man did not recognize her. He was walking stiffly down the road, looking straight ahead, and would have walked right past the dusty, dishevelled girl, had she not charged straight at his thin, shaky legs and clasped him round the waist.

'Sita!' he cried, when he had recovered his wind and his balance. 'Why are you here? How did you get off the island? I have been very worried—it has been bad, these last two days . . .'

'Is Grandmother all right?' asked Sita.

But even as she spoke, she knew that Grandmother was no longer with them. The dazed look in the old man's eyes told her as much. She wanted to cry—not for Grandmother, who could suffer no more, but for

Grandfather, who looked so helpless and bewildered. She did not want him to be unhappy. She forced back her tears and took his gnarled and trembling hand, and with Vijay walking beside her, led the old man down the crowded street.

She knew, then, that it would be on her shoulder that Grandfather would lean in the years to come.

They decided to remain in Shahganj for a couple of days, staying at a dharamsala—a wayside rest house—until the flood waters subsided. Grandfather still had two of the goats—it had not been necessary to sell more than one—but he did not want to take the risk of rowing a crowded boat across to the island. The river was still fast and dangerous.

But Vijay could not stay with Sita any longer.

'I must go now,' he said. 'My father and mother will be very worried and they will not know where to look for me. In a day or two the water will go down, and you will be able to go back to your home.'

'Perhaps the island has gone forever,' said Sita.

'It will be there,' said Vijay. 'It is a rocky island. Bad for crops but good for a house!'

'Will you come?' asked Sita.

What she really wanted to say was, 'Will you come to see me?' but she was too shy to say it; and besides, she wasn't sure if Vijay would want to see her again.

'I will come,' said Vijay. 'That is, if my father gets me another boat!'

As he turned to go, he gave her his flute.

'Keep it for me,' he said. 'I will come for it one day.' When he saw her hesitate, he smiled and said, 'It is a good flute!'

The Return

There was more rain, but the worst was over, and when Grandfather and Sita returned to the island, the river was no longer in spate.

Grandfather could hardly believe his eyes when he saw that the tree had disappeared—the tree that had seemed as permanent as the island, as much a part of his life as the river itself had been. He marvelled at Sita's escape.

'It was the tree that saved you,' he said.

'And the boy,' said Sita.

'Yes, and the boy.'

She thought about Vijay and wondered if she would ever see him again. Would he, like Phambiri and Hukam Singh, be one of those people who arrived as though out of a fairy tale and then disappeared silently and mysteriously? She did not know it then, but some of the moving forces of our lives are meant to touch us briefly and go their way . . .

And because Grandmother was no longer with them, life on the island was quite different. The evenings were sad and lonely.

But there was a lot of work to be done, and Sita did not have much time to think of Grandmother or Vijay or the world she had glimpsed during her journey.

For three nights they slept under a crude shelter made out of gunny bags. During the day, Sita helped Grandfather rebuild the mud hut. Once again they used the big rock for support.

The trunk which Sita had packed so carefully had not been swept off the island, but water had got into it and the food and clothing had been spoilt. But Grandfather's hookah had been saved, and in the evenings, after work was done and they had eaten their light meal which Sita prepared, he would smoke with a little of his old contentment and tell Sita about other floods which he had experienced as a boy. And he would tell her about the wrestling matches he had won, and the kites he had flown.

Sita planted a mango seed in the same spot where the peepul tree had stood. It would be many years before it grew into a big tree, but Sita liked to imagine herself sitting in the branches, picking the mangoes straight from the tree and feasting on them all day.

Grandfather was more particular about making a vegetable garden, putting down peas, carrots, gram and mustard.

One day, when most of the hard work had been done and the new hut was ready, Sita took the flute which had been given to her by Vijay, and walked down to the water's edge and tried to play it. But all she could produce were a few broken notes, and even the goats paid no attention to her music.

Sometimes Sita thought she saw a boat coming down the river, and she would run to meet it; but usually there was no boat, or if there was, it belonged to a stranger or to another fisherman. And so she stopped looking out for boats.

Slowly, the rains came to an end. The flood waters had receded, and in the villages people were beginning to till the land again and sow crops for the winter months. There were more cattle fairs and wrestling matches. The days were warm and sultry. The water in the river was no longer muddy, and one evening

Grandfather brought home a huge mahseer, and Sita made it into a delicious curry.

Deep River

Grandfather sat outside the hut, smoking his hookah. Sita was at the far end of the island, spreading clothes on the rocks to dry. One of the goats had followed her. It was the friendlier of the two, and often followed Sita about the island. She had made it a necklace of coloured beads.

She sat down on a smooth rock, and as she did so, she noticed a small bright object in the sand near her feet. She picked it up. It was a little wooden toy—a coloured peacock, God Krishna's favourite bird—it must have come down on the river and been swept ashore on the island. Some of the paint had been rubbed off; but for Sita, who had no toys, it was a great find.

There was a soft footfall behind her. She looked round, and there was Vijay, barefoot, standing over her and smiling.

'I thought you wouldn't come,' said Sita.

'There was much work in my village. Did you keep my flute?'

'Yes, but I cannot play it properly.'

'I will teach you,' said Vijay.

He sat down beside her and they cooled their feet in the water, which was clear now, taking in the blue of the sky. They could see the sand and the pebbles of the riverbed.

'Sometimes the river is angry and sometimes it is kind,' said Sita.

'We are part of the river,' said Vijay.

It was a good river, deep and strong, beginning in the mountains and ending in the sea.

Along its banks, for hundreds of miles, lived millions of people, and Sita was only one small girl among them, and no one had ever heard of her, no one knew her—except for the old man, and the boy, and the water that was blue and white and wonderful.

Read More in Puffin

Mr Oliver's Diary
Ruskin Bond
Illustrated by Anjali Nayar

A gun-toting, violin-playing Headmaster.
A homicidal barber.
A hungry leopard and about a hundred frogs on the loose.
Boys with a talent for pranks and jokes.
Ruskin Bond's fresh new school stories are a non-stop laugh riot.

Mr Oliver, a history teacher, arrives in Simla with a train-load of hungry boys to start a new term at the Prep School. As he records the antics of the amazing characters there, and all that they get up to, we quickly realize that there is never a dull moment. A fire, a missing Headmaster, runaway students make sure not a day goes by when Mr Oliver has nothing to report in his diary. He writes about the eccentric teachers, the girls' school next door and the lovely Anjali Ramola, whom he secretly admires.

Laugh-out-loud funny, with a core of old-world charm that is trademark Bond, *Mr Oliver's Diary* has stories and characters that have never appeared anywhere before. With his runaway wig, pet shrew and endearing dry wit, Mr Oliver is sure to become as well loved as those other vintage Ruskin Bond characters, Uncle Ken and Rusty.

Read More in Puffin

The Parrot Who Wouldn't Talk and Other Stories
Ruskin Bond
Illustrated by Kavita Arvind

I think everyone has at least one eccentric aunt or uncle in the family. I had more than one. My boyhood days were enlivened by their presence.

India's best-loved children's writer Ruskin Bond introduces us to some of the most endearing and adorable characters he has ever written about—his grandfather, with his unusual ability to disguise himself as the street-vendor, carpenter and sometimes the washerman; the eccentric and ubiquitous Uncle Ken, with his knack for trouble and disastrous escapades; the stationmaster Mr Ghosh and his amazing family comprising a dozen mice; and the unforgettable Aunt Ruby, whose encounter with a parrot who wouldn't talk will make you burst with laughter!

Meet the regimental myna, read about the snake who turned into a handsome prince every night, and enjoy the tale of the author's travails as a cook . . .

Heartwarming, funny and delightful, *The Parrot Who Wouldn't Talk and Other Stories* features some old favourites as well as refreshingly new stories written exclusively for this collection. Marked by Bond's inimitable style and trademark humour, and embellished with lively illustrations, this book will be a firm favourite with children.

Read More in Puffin

Panther's Moon and Other Stories
Ruskin Bond
Illustrated by Suddhasattwa Basu

He heard something scratching at the door, and the hair on his head felt tight and prickly. It was like a cat scratching, only louder. The door creaked a little whenever it felt the impact of the paw . . . 'It's the panther,' Bisnu muttered under his breath, sitting up on the hard floor.

Ten unforgettable tales of fascinating human encounters with animals and birds—of a man-eater that terrorizes an entire village; a strange and wonderful trust that develops between a fierce leopard and a boy; revengeful monkeys who never forgive a woman who grows dahlias; a crow who genuinely thinks human beings are stupid; and many others—creating a world in which men and wild creatures struggle to survive despite each other: a world where, in the end, one is not quite sure which side one is on.

Another marvellous collection of stories from India's most-loved author that will once again amuse, enchant and delight children of all ages.

Read More in Puffin

The Room of Many Colours:
A Treasury of Stories for Children
Ruskin Bond
Illustrated by Tapas Guha

For over five decades, Ruskin Bond has written charming tales that have mesmerized readers of all ages. This collection brings together his finest stories for children in one volume. Published previously as *A Treasury of Stories for Children*, this attractive rejacketed edition includes two new stories, 'The Big Race' and 'Remember this Day'.

Filled with a rich cast of characters and superb illustrations, *The Room of Many Colours: A Treasury of Stories for Children* is the definitive book for all Ruskin Bond fans and truly a collector's item.